# FRANKENSTEIN

The Frankenstein Series

## A.D WAYNE

In accordance with Australian copyright laws (1968) the scanning, uploading, and electronic sharing of any part of this book without the permission of the publisher constitute unlawful piracy and theft of the author's intellectual property and can incur legal action. If you would like to use material from the book (other than for review purposes), prior written permission must be obtained by the publisher who can be contacted at wild.dreams.publishing@gmail.com. Thank you for your support of the author's rights.

This book is a work of fiction. References to historical events, real people, or real locals are used fictitiously. Other names, characters, places and incidents are the product of the author's imagination, and any resemblance to actual events, locales or persons, living or dead, is entirely coincidental.

Wild Dreams Publishing
A publication of Wild Dreams Publishing
Traralgon, Vic
© 2020 by A.D Wayne
All rights reserved, including the right of reproduction in whole or in part in any form.
Wild Dreams Publishing is a registered trademark of Wild Dreams Publishing.
Manufactured in Australia.
All rights reserved.
Cover © A.D Wayne

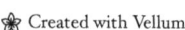 Created with Vellum

*For my beloved husband who loves me despite my twisted mind and dreams. For you maman, who inspired me to follow my dream. To you, grandpa, an angel in heaven, I love you.*

*This novel is dedicated to all who believed in me. I also dedicated it to those who doubted my will power, as it pushed me to prove them all wrong.*

# ACKNOWLEDGMENTS

This novel is a reflection of a part of me that dreams of a better tomorrow that might never come.

People who suffer from PTSD, chronic anxiety, OCD, phobias, among other mental illnesses must be warned that this novel contains it all. I refused not to share a darker part of myself. I want to break the stereotype and prove that it's not because we are scared that we cannot be strong.

Welcome to a dark world of mine where space and time are alive.

# I'M ALL OUT OF BUBBLEGUM

"Are you fucking insane, Frankie! We don't have time!"

"You fucking tell them we don't have time to shoot them!"

Frankie fell on her knees, and grabbed two plasma guns before sliding below the retractable door on the bridge of the enemy's ship. She quickly jumped on her feet, and started shooting at anything with a white, almost translucent skin, and ran toward the two crew members that were left behind, grabbed by those Rakes. She had come to despise them more than anything else in her life.

The walls were dark, the lighting very minimal, and the grid she ran on made more noises than the breathing of the ones she shot, incapable of a full vocal cry. Frankie grabbed one of the Rakes, his mouth fully opened, and about to scratch her shoulders. She put the plasma gun in his mouth, and shot. She then used him or her, because to be honest, Frankie knew there was no way to tell the females apart from the males, as an organic shield, and charged into the pack of Rakes coming her way.

Her guns almost out of fuel, she decided to retrieve one of the oxygen tanks from the side wall, and threw it among the Rakes before shooting. The explosion was contained once she ran out of the section, and closed the pressuring doors. She stopped, and bent over, hands on her knees, and took a deep breath. She then wiped her sweat dripping from her nose with the back of her right hand. Still holding a gun in each hand she looked to her side where she had to keep going, and started jogging.

The ship now seemed entirely emptied, and she got a message on her earpiece, "Frank! Answer me! We heard an explosion, are you, all right?

# A.D WAYNE

For fuck sake, Frank answer!" She turned on her vocal emitter, and said, "Yes, I caused the explosion." Her superior officer, Commander King, had orders to keep Frankie safe at all costs, and right now, she was several hundred meters away from him in a ship full of very hungry Rakes, "How the fuck do you suggest coming back? You blew up the only passage to their working teleportal beam!"

Frankie, with a cool tone in her voice, answered, "It was a risk I was willing to take." The Commander didn't find it one bit amusing, "That's funny, because see I am the Commander, and you're the Lieutenant. I make the decision, you follow my orders." Frankie followed a curving corridor, and decided to slow down, "Yeah, well I came here to chew bubblegum, and kick ass. I have two plasma guns with a few shots left, and no bubblegum. You do the math."

Frankie knew Commander Nakamo King wouldn't understand her reference. Nobody on her ship understood her puns from the twenty-first century, since she was the only one out of her timeline. She then turned off the device entirely. Frankie knew she would find her crewmates approaching the place where they were ambushed by Rakes, that according to King, weren't supposed to be onboard the abandoned ship. The air was heavy, and humid, the stink of the place burned inside Frankie's nostrils who wanted to beam out of the ship as soon as she could. But first, she had to free her men.

Frankie might not have been military material, or at least she thought so until saved by *Slicer*'s Captain. But she had proven herself time and time again. All those hours spent playing warfare video games were suddenly paying off, and helped protect herself from something she possessed that made her quite precious to the Captain of her ship.

The cries were loud, long, and agonizing. The mumbling, and what sounded like the chewing of animals crawled its way to Frankie's ears who feared what she was about to see when turning to the room on her right. She looked at her forearm bracer where it displayed a monitor screen of all *Slicer* members. She saw the faint life signs of her crewmates, and then turned on the 3D holographic blueprint of the ship, showing that on her left would be the feasting room.

She closed her eyes, knelt to the ground as slowly as she could, and crawled closer to the entrance of the room. Once opened, what she saw, created a sudden gag reflex. There was no more time to be discreet, as she threw up bile on herself. She jumped on her feet, and shot the two crewmates. Both of them hung from the ceiling by metallic hooks, resembling ones used by fishermen. It pierced through the bruised flesh on their backs. Denuded, the two men were hanging, their heads falling forwards. A wide X incision covered their abdomen, buckets at their feet, letting the blood drip down as Rakes exposed their tongues.

When Frankie saw the scene, she expected as much, but not for both crewmen to lift their heads up, orbits emptied from their eyeballs, and screaming without a tongue to articulate their pain. She shot them both between the eyes, and their heads fell forward instantly, putting them out of their misery. Twenty-eight Rakes came forward, angry, as they showed their long curving claws perfect to grip their prey as she stepped back. Frankie analyzed the situation rapidly, and calculated her chances of survival if she ran through the ship. "*9%. Not high enough.*" She thought to herself. She needed another strategy.

Frankie noticed a tall man with a black uniform, and helmet covering his head. Impossible to see through, she blinked, and hoped her ocular scanning lenses took a picture. She noticed his belt with a scarab looking device attached to it. "You'll have to do mate!" She propelled herself onto the man, elbowed his head, and then his stomach before injecting herself with the decoding serum, and entered the code, "Sextans A, NGC 3115, *Slicer* LSS, Authorization Code o5bw3d."

Frankie shot at the Rakes coming her way, until she felt her body dematerializing, leaving a sensation of absolute relaxation. Then everything disappeared until she felt stretched out into a tube, and instantly rematerialized.

"What was the idea, Lieutenant Stein?"

"Yes, I'm happy I'm alive too."

"Lieutenant!"

Frankie got back on her feet. The man covered in a black military suit was about to lift himself up, so Frankie kicked his head, and knocked him out for the third time. She walked down the circular Decoder pedestal, holding her head with one hand. She was covered in soot, and sweating like she just went for a hundred-kilometer marathon. King was yelling at her. She had to follow his orders when away on missions. Then Frankie felt shivers grabbing onto her spine, crawling its way to the back of her neck when he walked in the room.

"Lieutenant Stein, what is this Khe soldier doing on my ship?"

It seemed as if Frankie lost her words, the entire language indeed. She walked back to the Khe soldier, grabbed his teleportal device, also known as a PBU, and unlocked his helmet. She then caught on to its ocular lenses on his eyeballs, and retrieved the chip placed in his bracer. She walked down the Decoder, and handed it to Captain Caldwell, who had turned forty-nine years old the week before.

"This Khe soldier was the relic we were looking for." Frankie admitted, "I read his signature when we teleported to the supposedly abandoned ship." She mentioned slowly looking at her superior officer with a frown as he affirmed the wrecked ship deserted by the crew. "These objects, once I analyze them, will prove to be the missing parts of previous encoded Grey artifacts left behind. It also proves our theory of the Rakes working alongside the Dome...um...Sir."

Frankie looked down when her Captain asked with his grave, and commanding voice, "How were you able to use the PBU? You needed access to a Rake code." Frankie wasn't about to reveal all of her secrets to her Captain, and so she answered, "As for the Portable Beaming Unit, I...um" She cleared her throat before King said, "She disobeyed my orders, and went on a silly mission to—" Caldwell raised his hand before King, and uninterestingly nodded, his eyes fixed on Frankie, "Yes, yes, yes, subordination, who gives a fuck Commander. We're at war."

He had Frankie look into his eyes, "How did you get that code?" She had to think fast, "I hacked their system, and copied one of their codes when I knew a Khe soldier was onboard the ship." Captain Caldwell smiled, "Move the prisoner to the brig until Dr. Gillman can start the rehabilitation process." Before leaving the room, Caldwell glanced at Frankie one last time, subtly winked, and grinned before saying, "Good work, Lieutenant." Followed by, "Both of you take a shower, and report to Dr. Gillman."

Frankie couldn't help but smile, and with the objects in her hands, about to walk out, she felt King's grip on her shoulder. She knew he would again lecture her about how the Captain was a weirdo, and not to let him inside her head. He tried his best to have the Captain lose interest in Frankie, but it never worked. She would get away with many things, but then again, "I'm not a real soldier, Nakamo." She said.

They both walked toward the closest elevator to get to their quarters. Once inside the half-moon shaped cylinder elevator, King pressed the stop button, and Frankie suddenly felt a little claustrophobic. It had been over four years since she come onboard *Slicer*, four years that she had become close friends with King.

"Caldwell will be the end of you. He is dangerous. He is working his way into your head, Frankie."

"You are paranoid, Nakamo. It's been almost half a decade, Caldwell would be the slowest criminal of all time!"

King slowly approached Frankie, and moved a streak of her hair away from her face. Confused by the loving gesture, and admitting to herself that yes, she once had some indecent thoughts about him in the past, she tried resisting the softness of his touch. She looked into his black eyes as he said, "It's just that, if something would happen to you or if someone would take you away from me, I don't know if I could ever forgive myself." Quite a few inches more than a foot over her head, King leaned in, and Frankie thought about stopping him, but she secretly wanted it. It had been so long since a man caressed her skin, and kissed her. She craved the touch, the skin of a man against her own, and the pleasure it gave that she surprised herself by risking their friendship, when a monitor screen turned on, "Is everything all right? The elevator seems stuck."

The moment got away, and King replied by pressing a button, and moving his face in the camera's frame, "Yes, all is okay. Mind your own business, will ya." The silence was awkward, and Frankie knew it took a lot of courage for King to show weakness before her, and so she moved her hand to grab his, and said, "Maybe it's better that way." King rolled his eyes, "As long as he's in your head, I just have no chance." He left the elevator, and Frankie walked to her quarters thinking about what might have happened if there had not been any interruptions. Would they have stopped at kissing, or since she craved a man so much, would she have let him...? "Stop, this is insane. This whole situation is entirely insane!" She murmured out loud to herself while walking to her quarters in the opposite direction of Commander Nakamo King.

She wanted to turn around, and see if he looked at her, but it would break her heart if he did or didn't. Frankie thought of herself as foolish, she needed to focus on the reason why she was on *Slicer*. She had to think about her mission, and duty, and then, they appeared in her head. The door to her quarters opened to let her in, but Frankie was immobile. In her head, images of emptied eye orbits appeared, mouths without tongues, and her shooting...it just didn't go away.

# CLOSE ENCOUNTER

2100 Hours, September 14th, 2510
(Gregorian Calendar,)
Milky Way, Orion Quadrant, Rake Space,
*Slicer*, Medical Facility

In the year 2506, a young woman known as Frank N. Stein was brought onto a starship named *Slicer*. Despite the shock of coming face to face with aliens in the future, she joined the Alliance crew. Once on board, she lost all recollection of joining the fleet, and had one of her most deeply felt anxiety attacks. "It was one of the most horrifying episodes of my life. I was lucky you were present, Doctor. With those anti-anxiety shots, I was able to cope with a new reality better than I ever thought I could. I didn't know what I would've done without them." Frankie said, her hand rubbing against her forehead as she closed her eyes, and her fingers softly went down to her mouth. She couldn't stop thinking about her first interactions with the crew. Afraid, unaware of what was true or false.

"Captain Caldwell took great care of you." Dr. Gillman said as she served them both hot peppermint tea. "I remember when he came to me, and first mentioned you." She said with a smile, "He said he did not expect you to be that beautiful." Frankie did remember thinking the same when crossingCaldwell's eyes for the first time. Bright frosty blue, and feline shaped, a beautiful arched nose with lithe honeyed lips. She had a hard time containing her emotions when looking at him. Once the drugs kicked in, and she could finally take a deep breath, she recalled his touch on both her arms, letting her know that everything would be all right.

"Well, Doctor?" Frankie asked, standing up, drinking her tea while the doctor looked at her physical analysis result. "You are in perfect health. Ready for the mission, but if you'd prefer to stay here I can give you a leave of absence." Taking another sip of her tea, Frankie answered with a frown looking down, "It isn't necessary. I wish I was given more weaponry than just my fighting skills, and a few blades."

"I don't understand, Captain Caldwell never mentioned you going weaponless. It doesn't make sense."

"There is lots about him that don't make sense...he has obscure, and strange reasons that go beyond my own if you ask me."

Frankie left the medical facility after thanking Dr. Gillman for her tea. As she walked to her quarters, she recalled her first year on *Slicer*. The navy blue and dark grey nanofiber walls, with built-in monitor screens, somehow triggered her memory when she looked up, and saw the surveillance cameras placed every five meters on both sides. Throughout the first weeks of her adaptation on the starship more than four years ago, Frankie had many things to learn. Frankie disregarded the overwhelming feeling of finding herself in a 'sci-fi' situation. She often felt afraid of what could happen to her. Yet, she found herself quite accustomed to the ship, and recognized the technology surrounding her proving the theory that she carried this 'Grey gene.'

Frankie had everyone intrigued by her knowledge, and behavior. Many asked questions, but she had no answers. It was almost as if something had triggered a long-lost suppressed memory she had in her. Like something that had been given to her. Then, Frankie met a man named Nakamo King, and a young woman named Alaska Leclerc. They quickly became friends. All three being from Earth, their bond proved to be thicker, as humans seemed to be seen as weaker than most other species on board *Slicer*.

Frankie became determined to show the other aliens that they were wrong. However, sadly, for the first months aboard the starship that she now knew voyaged through time and space, she was told to remain onboard learning about the Alliance association. They were working on uniting a few planets together against their common enemy, The Dome. She had to also learn about the mission, and *Slicer*'s purpose.

"Lieutenant Stein, report to the war room."

"Yes, Sir." Frankie answered, snapping out of her daydream, and quickly changing direction to enter an elevator, "Deck 3." She replayed Caldwell's voice in her head over and over.

Caldwell, his strong, masterful voice with an accent reminiscent to one from Ireland had her weak to her knees. She tried not to think about him as much. But quickly, memories of her second year on board *Slicer* surfaced. Lost in her thoughts again, she was trying to tie up her deep midnight black hair, long to the base of her neck, her long bangs steadily falling back down hiding her forehead, Frankie was proudly showing her half sleeve tattoo of a lion coming out from the clouds. Frankie finally managed to tie up her hair, a few strands falling down her neck.

Three years ago...

"How do you like your new quarters, Miss Stein?" He stood right past the entrance to her new chambers. Both his arms on each side of his hips, she found him looking quite uncomfortable with his head leaning lower than usual.

"Please, just call me Frankie. I'm no Starfleet officer or anything."

"Starfleet?"

"Never mind."

Frankie wore loose dark grey lounge pants, and a grandpa scientist and his grandson cartoon tee. She looked at Caldwell, exhausted, and weary of all the studies that she had undertaken. Her only wish was to be alone, but when looking into the eyes of Caldwell, she thought maybe his company would be pleasing.

"I was told you have extensive knowledge of martial arts."

"I do." She said with much confidence, "My ex taught me all he knew about various martial arts. I wanted him to teach me and he did."

He might not have known the nerdy fandom native of the twenty-first century, but his eyes were still fixed on her when she asked what his intentions were when it came down to her presence on the ship. Frankie had not been told anything, other than to become accustomed to the ways of *Slicer*, but her learning was faster than they had ever seen, and so they had her jump from one station to the next at a speed the crew never thought possible for a human.

"You carry something that we thought never survived human DNA." His smile was hidden in the corner of his mouth, his brows raised as he spoke, left a few wrinkles carving in his forehead.

"What do you mean, I'm not pregnant or anything." Frankie affirmed with a chuckle before she heard Caldwell answer with a fine quick look at her from head to toe, and grinned, "I know."

Frankie was to be upgraded from a confined guest to another title she didn't know, and awaited Caldwell to bring up. "Since the beginning of time, experiments have been done by an alien species called the Greys a thousand times on humans, but never survived. You, Frankie, are known to be the only one to have it asleep within your DNA. Their gene is alive within you, but dormant." He walked toward her, both his hands apart as if to show no danger, "The Greys have tried to blend their genes with other species, none have worked. Except for you."

He was now inches from her body, her head aligned with his chest and she looked up, and he leaned his head down. They both looked at each other, and she felt something she had not felt in a long time... sexual. She asked what her new assignment would be. Caldwell answered, "You will be part of missions to retrieve what the Greys have left behind. We need to stop The Dome from conquering the Orion Quadrant, including your own solar system back in your own timeline of Alpha Earth."

Frankie had learned of The Dome. She knew they were invading different periods of her planet thus changing history most likely making it fit their agenda. Frankie was abducted by *Slicer* in time. The crew depended on her to translate Grey's inscriptions, and share the real human history, so they could restore it once their mission would be accomplished.

"Your first mission will be to accompany King, and Wolf aboard a starship wreck. We were able to read low human radio frequencies. It is normally attached to Grey's artifacts." His hand near her head, he seemed to want to touch her hair, and she wished he would, but she answered, "You want me to go on this mission?"

"As long as you do not get hurt."

Frankie had gone on many missions in the past two years. She had accomplished more as a newcomer to *Slicer* than any other member onboard the starship. King, and Wolf often being those she would perform operations with. Nakamo King was usually the one leading the mission crew, while Wolf was a good shot, he was also utilized because of his ability to assimilate languages at a breakneck pace. Some other crew members would tag along when needed, but the leading trio remained the same. Frankie had seen many perish through their relentless operations. Always delicate to accomplish, retrieving Grey's artifacts gathered by one race trying to take over the Orion Quadrant—the galaxy map divided by four, created by the Walrians ally, had Earth's solar system falling under Leo. The Rakes were part of the second quadrant, Scorpius.

*"The Rakes are an alien species known for their gruesome skill of capturing organic beings, and eating them alive. I know it doesn't sound as frightening said as such, but believe me, when seeing it before your own eyes–, and you will, it is a view that you will not soon forget, if ever."*

Frankie remembered King's words from their first mission onboard a Rakes' ship as if it had happened the day before, *"Never let your guard down Frankie, or it will be the end of you. Also, if you wonder why the Rakes are after the Greys' artifacts, Captain Caldwell suspects they might be working for the Dome."*

Her head down, walking toward the war room, Frankie played the scenario over, and over in her head. The Rakes attacking crew members with their claws, and their long, razor-sharp teeth, literally feeding off the person's flesh while he or she would be defending themselves. *So many dead, I lost count! How am I even still alive after all this shit?* Frankie kept walking, and another daydream surfaced.

# FRANKENSTEIN

Two years ago...

"YOU CANNOT EXPECT me to believe you want me to go on missions unarmed! Those are Rakes! I've studied everything about them, and yet, I'm told they are worse than described in your databank!" Frankie's voice was strong, affirmed, and despite being angry, sounded more authoritarian than she ever thought possible from her natural introverted nature. "Your Captain said he never wanted me to be hurt. How am I supposed to believe you?"

Frankie walked around Captain Caldwell's office on the bridge. The walls were black, and his desk seemed to be made of glass, but was of a very resistant material Frankie didn't know. There was a full horizontal monitor behind him keeping him up to date with what was going on with the bridge, and where they were heading. The lighting was soft, yet very efficient for such a dark room. On the Captain's desk was nothing but an integrated holographic computer, and an infinity statue made of titanium. There were no memories, no personal belongings, or decorations he received over his service in the Alliance or Liberty military.

"They might be right about you Admiral Heikki after all, you care about nothing. But what you are to gain? The Captain never told me to go on a mission without a weapon, yet you keep saying those are his orders."

Frankie looked at the display of Caldwell's Captain certificates from planet Liberty from the Gliese 581c star system's military. It was the one thing he was forced to display that was even remotely personal to him. Frankie then noticed three badges exposed below: A Cross of Valour, which meant he had been in peril, and despite about to lose his life he either chose to save his crew or carry on with his mission. Beside it was what seemed to resemble the Victoria Cross, she remembered from her uncle who got one. It meant that despite being in the presence of the enemy, he stood his ground, and sacrificed his own body, and mind for the mission he had to accomplish. Finally, she looked at the blue, and white medal with a fleur-de-lis, and associated it with his devotion to Liberty, its people, and community.

"How can someone as brave as him have to be under you?" Her eyes, half closed in confusion as she frowned, hugging herself, pulling on the sleeves of her white zipped hoodie. "You have insulted me for the last time, Lieutenant." Frankie was about to move from behind Caldwell's translucent desk, when she heard his commanding voice, soft-spoken, and heartfelt.

"I might have no choice but to follow your orders, but one day you'll be mine to toy with Admiral Heikki." Frankie knew the admiral would have something to say, to anyone else, but Frankie was too precious of an asset to reprimand. The automatic door to Caldwell's office opened to the starship's bridge. Caldwell had just ordered his pilot, Erik Madsen, to maintain their position so the away team could leave. His arms were straight on both sides, but Frankie noticed he was playing with his cuticles. His military suit on, charcoal grey pants with sides of silver, a black tee under his opened dark vest with silver lines down the shoulders to the wrists. His rank was exposed beneath the Alliance emblem, the everlasting three main Egyptian pyramids.

"Whatever you think about doing to Captain Caldwell right now, don't. He is spoken for already." Frankie answered with a strong voice pointing at him, "Yet, his ring finger shows no sign of a ring or lack of tan. So, whatever you think you are restraining me from doing, don't get your hopes up."

A little run of air brought Caldwell's musky scent to Frankie, and he embraced her. He then looked at her and said, "What are you still doing here, Lieutenant? The away team is waiting for you in the Decoder room."

Twenty-five missions later, and Frankie was still unarmed, and her 'Grey gene' had not kicked in yet. She thought the Admiral either had too much power or wanted her dead. Although proven to be deadlier than a plasma gun, Frankie owed it to her training given to her by her ex, and not the alien factor of her DNA. She approached the room, and when about to go in, she took a deep breath, and hummed, *"Never free, never me...so I dub thee unforgiven."*

The sliding door opened, and she walked into the war room. The blue lights were on, and helped with seeing the holograms clearly. It showed another vessel that was abandoned by the Rakes. It seemed to have been through better days. The starship belonging to those flesh-eating enemies were often in the shape of the tip of an arrow. Grafted onto the exterior hull were patches of skin from their enemies, and when zooming to see the condition, buckets of blood had been dumped all over its exterior. However, that one had a large, and full flag recognizable for Frankie, "The Jolly-Roger...I thought last time was a coincidence, but this has to be more than that. It means something."

Of course, King, Wolf, and Leclerc asked what a Jolly-Roger was, while Captain Caldwell frowned and showed confusion along with Dr. Gillman. "In Earth's history—despite it coming from the Templars, it was borrowed in the Age of Piracy. This flag was flown when a pirate ship was about to attack." Frankie added blowing up the image of the skull in front of two crossing bones, "The Rakes are either aware of ancient human history, or they have cracked through a Grey's artifact, or, they are letting you know they are aware of me being on board your ship."

Captain Caldwell paced around, but ordered for the mission to carry on regardless of Frankie's intervention clearly stating, "This is a trap. We are walking right into it." Then he asked how she would know, "Because this is the oldest trick in the pirate book. Look injured, lead them to you, then take everything, and give nothing back." The Captain chose to ignore her warning, and sent the mission team away on the Rakes' ship. It barely took two minutes to walk down their Decoder, once at the door of the room to walk to their tenth deck's hallway, Frankie felt someone holding her from behind. Her mouth was covered, and when she was about to jab her elbow into the Rake's ribcage, she felt a needle down her throat, and her eyes closed.

"Dear Frankenstein, it's time to wake up!" A small, sneering voice said while Frankie desperately tried to open her eyes. Everything appeared foggy at first. She tried to lift her arm to help rub her eyes, but she was restrained. "It's only for precaution, the procedure is a little painful."

Still waking up from the drug she was attacked with, Frankie feared for her life in many ways, and blamed herself for the kidnapping that should have never occurred if she would have shown more focus. She opened her eyes widely, and finally as if something triggered a switch in her mind, she saw clearer than she ever had before. She saw one of her crewmates at the back of a cargo room. He was tied upside down, shirtless, and his arms held to his hips by ropes. Punctures were eminent going down his chest, she could hear him choking. "It's taking too much time!" One of the members growled a little and then with one quick slash to his throat, an overflow of blood fell in a large bucket. It was too big, and significant for one body, and she looked past the crewman, and saw the bodies of other *Slicer* officers that had been sent to the ship, lifeless, and obviously emptied as well.

*I'm still on the Rakes' ship, about to suffer the same fate...wait, he said procedure. What procedure?* She looked at the one who had spoken to her a moment earlier. He wore a tight black vinyl suit, reflecting a spectacular light each time he crossed the projector above. *He doesn't look like a Rake. He must be from the Dome or working for them...what's their name again...they're known for their torture taste, the Ensians!*

The overly tall, and slim male had a table with many surgical tools. The alien wore a face covering porcelain looking Venetian mask. It was held on his head by a black veil, while the mask itself had an inhumanly wide smile painted on it. His elongated thin fingers grabbed on to a scalpel, and he approached Frankie with a skip of his feet. "There is a choice for you, Frankenstein," he said with his adenoidal voice, "You either accept to work for the Dome, and give us the coordinates of *Slicer,* or I steal the information from your frontal lobes, and then might jump to the frontal cortex, and hippocampus as we know the human brain needs both to recollect long-term memories."

Frankie squeezed her lips, and gathered saliva before spitting on the mask of the Ensians' surgeon. "Knock yourself out, I don't respond well to coercion, and even less to bullies." She frowned, and played along as if she knew all about her Grey gene, and even how to use it because they seemed unaware of her condition, *I don't even believe I own anything from them, so good luck clown face.* "Argh!" Frankie cried at the top of her lungs when her eyes covered in tears, and her mouth opened more extensive than ever, warm, velvety liquid dripping down her abdomen, she felt the surgical tool right between her ribs as the surgeon twisted it.

"Changed your mind, yet?"

"I don't know, you tell me. Go fuck yourself!" Frankie responded as she spat blood over the holes where his bright yellow veiny eyes were.

The tool fell to the ground, and the surgeon screamed for an antibacterial rag to disinfect his mask. It was clear to Frankie, though in throbbing pain, and losing blood at an alarming rate, that the Ensians were germaphobic, almost exactly like her, and that they apparently thought her Grey gene was not a gene, but a memory. Otherwise, they would've used her saliva when she spat, a hair, or her blood.

"Dead, I'm of no use to you." She retorted, trying to understand why they would try to kill her, "At this rate, I'll be dead in six minutes."

"You think we don't have reanimation chambers at the Dome?" The Ensian answered, angrier than ever when planting another scalpel into her leg.

"I'm sure you've heard this all the time, shithead, but make sure I don't come out of this alive, or I swear that I'll go full Dark Ages on your ass."

The surgeon then commanded to be handed a device that looked like a remote. He pressed a button, and a laser turned on. He was able to direct it through a joystick, and a monitor he would look at on his left. One of the nurses, dressed like him but in a different color wearing the same mask, covered in realistically painted scars, asked with a juvenile small voice, "Then, why not use the Dolos glove, Doctor? He said with a focus on the laser, "It has been tried before, but she has a powerful mind. This is our last resort. She might not come out of it useful, but, I will erase everything, and feed her to the Dome."

Yet, Frankie had next to no recollection of being under torture by the Ensians before. Memories might have been suppressed, she guessed. She should've been horrified by the laser, but the loss of blood had her very dizzy, and overcome by weariness. She stared at the laser, she wanted to fight, but there was no more strength in her. To what end? Her crew was dead. She thought about Wolf, and King, and hoped their end was quick, and painless.

The laser hit her skull, and heated its way through. She screamed until her voice cracked, and no more air filled her lungs. Tears rolled down her face. Just when she felt like it was the end, she heard the doors being knocked down with hefty echoes banging through on the reinforced metal. Then she listened to a pressurized mechanism being forced, and saw Caldwell coming in with a plasma gun.

The surgeon turned to the Captain, and with his head tilted, both his hands apart from his face he said, "Zad-yreL...still alive, I see." It was with an authoritative, and icy voice that he answered, "I'm Captain Jason Namito Caldwell." The surgeon didn't sound amused, "Yes, yes, let's not open that wound again...shall we?"

"You hurt Frank N. Stein. That was a big mistake."

"Oops." A sneered laugh, "If she's to be of no use to us, neither will she be to you,

Zad-yreL!"

All Frankie felt was a zap, like an electrical disruption in her brain, and all turned entirely black. A few echoes fading, and Captain Caldwell's voice disappeared when she mumbled, "Jay..."

# HOME AGAIN

0200 Hours, September 15th, 2510
(Gregorian Calendar)
Milky Way, Orion Quadrant,
Rake Space, *Slicer*
Medical Facility

Her body felt heavy, and she could barely open her eyes. She touched her forehead with the base of the palm of her hand, and tried to remember what happened. It was all a blur. Nothing made sense. Frankie was not aboard an enemy's spaceship, it couldn't be! She finally found the strength to open her eyes, and saw the white comforter covering her, she felt at least two fluffy pillows, and, on the side, on a table, she saw a metallic vase with white lilies.

"Captain Caldwell had them sent for you. He said they were your favorites."

Dr. Gillman, Frankie was onboard *Slicer*. She felt tears in her eyes, and wiped them off. She then stared at the lilies, and tried to recall the first time she mentioned her favorite flowers to the Captain. Frankie then felt something warm on her left side, at the height of her thigh. She turned her attention to it, and saw a little fur ball. It had caramel-colored fur, a long body, arms proportional to its height, and a long rigid tail. The fur on its belly was paler than on its back, while its face was almost like an eggshell white, and its ears were of a darker brown just like around its eyes. Frankie asked Dr. Gillman what a meerkat was doing sleeping in the bed she was in.

"Well, it sometimes happens that one's wife gets a pet on an away mission without asking her spouse if she is allergic to a hateful creature who tried to eat her face." Gillman explained with a smile that suggested her uncomfortable situation with her wife as she was applying the cream on her right cheek, "Bottom line is, meerkats could be the death of me, and that one wants me dead."

Gillman explained that because the medical facility was sterile, and had prepared allergy medicine, she brought the meerkat in "Almost instantly, that thing from hell escaped me, not without scratching the hell out of my hands, and face, and ran to your bed. He's been at your side ever since. Also, I believe it's a male."

After adding that the meerkat was of no threat to her or any of the patients as the air was always being cleaned by a sophisticated air filtering system that eliminated allergens as it came in. So, keeping the medical area impeccable for patients attending it, Dr. Gillman wondered if Frankie would keep the meerkat.

"Of course, I would, but I barely remember who I am or where I am. I can't recall anything that happened hours ago. I mean...is this my home?"

"It is, it has been for over four years. Don't you remember, Frankie?"

Pointing to the other side, Dr. Gillman presented two people of somewhat not too alien in appearance. "Alaska?" Frankie said with a warm smile as she sat beside her, and held her hand in hers. She had the greenest eyes she had ever seen, pale purple-greyish skin, blue tattooed hieroglyphs on her forehead, chin, and both cheeks. Her jet-black bob haircut had two strands of her hair in the front coming together when she looked down at Frankie. "I don't know what happened, all I know is that I was scared, and...I'm unsure of what happened to me."

Then, she looked at the tall man with golden skin walking forward. He had dark hair tied in one long braid, and eyes as dark as the pit of the night. He wore a sports grey tank top, and said with a silvery voice, "I've never wanted for this to happen, Frankie. It went wrong. You were right, it was a trap, but Caldwell didn't listen to you." Frankie tried to remember, but nothing seemed to surface in her mind. She knew his name was Nakamo King, but that was all she could recall of him. "It happened to you once before." The tall man said, "You lost all memories of us, you forgot all about your life with us a year ago." Frankie thought he looked Native American, maybe he was? "This time, it seems that you have somewhat adapted, and Dr. Gillman said she'll be able to give you your memories back."

Alaska helped Frankie to remember the last mission by mentioning she on board a Rake pirate ship. "It had the Jolly-Roger flag graphed on it. You were zapped, like a shock through your brain, and you twitched," then Frankie remembered. "I was tied to a table." Her eyes closed, she still felt the presence of the doctor, and King close to her, another shock, "I was behind Nakamo, and Wolf when we teleported." She opened her eyes in fright, "Wolf!"

Frankie could almost remember the mission now, although it seemed to be a blur, and a puzzle to put back together. She remembered Wolf was there with them. Then, a crewman that was being bled alive tied upside down, so his blood fell down a bucket. A pile of corpses behind him. "Draca!"

Dr. Gillman touched her leg, "It's okay, Lieutenant Draca Wolf is over there." She pointed on the other side of the room. "He will be fine. He was only shot at the bottom of the spine. His paralysis won't be permanent. Olymnu is a regenerative species. He only needs to spend a few hours laying down in the sarcophagus." Agitated, trying to fight off the hands of Alaska and King, now on the other side of her bed, Frankie remembered the scene. She decided to move out of the bed to see Wolf for herself, somehow feeling guilty about what happened yet, unable to recall anything past the drug injection she got on the side of her throat.

"We were an LSS crew, it was a dangerous mission with only members of different times," King explained, but left Frankie confused as to what LSS meant. "Liberty Star Ship. The Alliance believe we are still part of the ATS, Alliance Temporal Starship. It is the name of the guild that allied all planets united against the Dome, and those who... captured you for the second time, i.e. the Rakes because of the Captain. It's enough for now." The entire facility now smelled like the lilies that the Captain had sent her. She wanted to know why she was on a mission when she barely remembered being military. "You're not, Frankie. You're...special." Alaska said, clearly wanting to keep her in a good mental state. "I'm damaged, I know I am." Frankie stated.

Her eyes fixed in the bright emerald of Alaska's gaze, she heard her crystal voice say, "You are not damaged, Frankie. You're perfect. You're human, like Nakamo, and me. We're humans, and we're stronger than anyone thinks. You've proven that time, and time again." The words, the passion, and strength in her grip reminded Frankie that they were more than friends, they were family. They made themselves family. King added with his kind voice, "Somehow, the Captain, or the Admiral thought it to be wise to keep sending you on missions unarmed. I don't care, I blame Caldwell. I revolted against him, but he threatened to have you moved to another team, and I couldn't let that happen. I don't trust

## A.D WAYNE

anyone else than Wolf, Alaska, and myself to keep you safe...despite your obvious knowledge in self-defence that saved our asses more than once. I won't have you move to another team. Not on my watch."

It was hard for Frankie to remember Captain Caldwell's words, when all she could recall of him was his touch, his arms around her, and his affection toward her. Again, memories were zapping in, and out of her mind. Hearing his words, *"...if I lose you...I don't know what I would do."* Did he love her? On her way to ask Alaska about her relationship status with Caldwell, she heard a masterful, and grave voice asking from a monitor speaker, "Dr. Gillman, how is our patient?" The reptilian looking doctor answered with an assured voice, carefully looking at Frankie who stared back with certain anxiety, realizing that she had lost all memories of her presence aboard the *Slicer* in the past four years.

"Miss Stein is awake now, but sadly she has no specific recollection past a certain time, despite showing signs of incomprehensible resistance to mind control. Miss Stein seems to remember certain things, recent events mostly. Someone voluntarily cut the connection between her frontal cortex, and hippocampus before she was brought to me. The torture seemed not to have been remembered so far."

Frankie sat up straight on the bed, and moved her feet beneath her. She held her new meerkat close to her chest, and asked what Dr. Gillman was talking about, but she interrupted Frankie answering the Captain, "I've detected the stopping process of consolidation by small pulses of electroshock. It was very precise, and almost undetectable...I suspect the Calvanian are behind this method. The Ensians' methodology is too flawed." Frankie moved straight on her knees, still holding her new pet close to her, but quickly King, and Alaska held her back, and tried to calm her down when she heard the Captain of the ship once again, "Will you be able to fix Miss Stein's memory, Dr. Gillman, and has your research proven your theory, right?"

Through the speaker placed by Frankie's bed, that somehow sounded like a surround system, she could hear his voice clearly. To satisfy her curiosity, Frankie turned her head, and looked at him on a screen above the speaker. She stopped moving, her eyes cleared up slightly from tears of fright as she looked into his frosty hooded eyes that showed creases around them. His skin was fair, and his black hair cut in a short businessman fashion, but as the front had longer streaks, two fell down on one side of his face.

"Yes, Captain. It is possible for me to reanimate Miss Stein's memories by reconnecting the neurons that were tampered with. As for my hypothesis on creating an organic shield around Miss Stein's brain, it is doable by awakening her telepathic, and telekinesis abilities that are at this stage of the twenty-first's century humanoid evolution still dormant, but might be increased by her Grey gene."

Sitting on her bed, moving her eyes back and forth between Dr. Gillman, and the strange ship's Captain, Frankie listened to the conversation as if she was a ghost about to be thrown back into her body in the most undesirable way. She thought for a moment that nobody could see her, or that she has been bought by that Captain!

"So, Miss Stein's Grey gene is awakening?"

"Yes, and at a rapid pace I may add."

"So, this means she was—"

"Yes. She was abducted between the time of her mother's pregnancy to her fifth year of existence. It is hard to say. Miss. Stein does have the gene allowing her to control certain outside environments, thus capable of creating an organic shield, much like the Earth's magnetic poles, which protects it against solar flares."

Frankie then knew what needed to be talked about. She held her meerkat closer, but he moved around her neck. Frankie had both her hands on the mattress as she crawled forward to look at Dr. Gillman, holding her tablet over her chest with one hand while placing her glasses back in place with the other. The glasses, Frankie noticed, projected her medical file while moving from data file to data file according to Gillman's eye blinks.

"How will the procedure be done, Doctor?"

"I will place Miss Stein in an artificially induced coma, and first reconnect the severed neurons. Then, I will attempt to lower her life signs as much as possible, and activate the gene with electro pulses. If that doesn't work, I will send in her bloodstream the nano-spiders to safely guide them to target the gene itself."

Frankie couldn't believe what she was hearing. Something had to be wrong. This could not be real. No one showed any concern, not even King or Alaska. No one cared about her health at all or if she would stay on the table, and never awaken again. It sounded like a very dangerous procedure, and despite her desire to remember everything, she didn't know if cutting her skull open was necessary.

"How certain are you of Miss Stein's recovery, doctor?"

"One hundred percent sure. Stein's life is in no danger at all. It is a very minor procedure for a doctor of my caliber."

"All right, Dr. Gillman. You have my permission to proceed."

Frankie was about to shout, when she heard the Captain say something that caught her attention very effectively. She had no intention of losing that memory. Because at that moment, something strange awakened inside of her. Something she didn't know she could feel.

"I'll be on standby to hear from you when she awakens." He stopped, his voice lowered, and with a subtle growl he said, "If you miscalculated anything, Dr. Gillman, you will be teleported outside my main viewer window, and I'll watch you turn inside out as your blood boils inside your veins."

"Understood, Captain Caldwell."

Frankie spoke aloud, "I'm here! Does anyone see me?" She grimaced, and waved her hands over her head as she frowned, "Don't I have a say in all this? We're talking about my fucking brain, here!" She shouted louder as she moved before the viewer to attack the Captain with the worse she could throw at him, "Have you ever heard of 'My fucking body, my fucking damn rules!' You fucking shithead, you think—"

Her hair was a mess, her meerkat popped his head from behind her right ear, and her eyes, she guessed, were red, and puffy from all the crying. But she looked at him with a vision ready to shoot bullets when he replied with a soft voice, after the gasps following her language to the Captain, "Tutankhaten." Her body suddenly felt more substantial than a metric ton, her eyes were closing as she felt herself falling onto the mattress. She heard her meerkat squeaking but couldn't do anything. When her head touched the pillows, surrounding the place where she had laid before, she listened to what was left of the conversation between the Captain, and Dr. Gillman. As if everything was moving in slow motion, Frankie tried to move, but her body was not responsive to her command. Afraid, she hoped her new pet would be okay. She felt him move on the back of her neck, hiding in her hair. She listened to the conversation flowing around her.

"Dr. Gillman, I expect this subliminal word not to work after your operation, and be sure that I will test it first-hand."

"Understood."

"And doctor, you better make sure she remembers everything, and when I say everything, I mean from her birth to this second now. Am I making myself clear?"

"Yes, Sir."

"All right. Go to work. Caldwell out."

Why was it so important to the Captain that she recovered all of her memories, even those that she knew were suppressed? It was becoming harder, and harder for Frankie to think straight. She could barely make out what the Doctor, and Captain were saying. But now that they were done talking, she feared for her life, and yet, she felt strong hands moving her from the ground as her meerkat crawled on her chest.

"She is fighting the subliminal effect! How can she do that?" One of the male nurses asked the doctor while she was examining the medical instruments by the operating table. Frankie was being placed on the operating table. Immobile, and unable to speak, she could only listen to the conversation between Dr. Gillman, and her nurses.

"She has the Grey gene. She can fight anything with her mind at will if she wants, and I will help her get there faster." Her voice was monotone, and focused. Frankie wondered if she would get her skull sliced, and end up with a scar, and stitches on her forehead like the real Frankenstein's Monster. Then a hasty, and curious female voice was heard while putting on a mask over her mouth.

"But she's just a twenty-first-century human, it's not supposed to be awakened yet! It's not even supposed to have worked at all!"

"That's why Captain Caldwell sent us to get her more than four years ago. Obviously, the Greys felt like her DNA was worth testing, and they were right to think so."

Frankie was finally able to open her eyes, slightly, but she saw a circle with twelve bulbs of light. It reminded her of something...something from a very long time ago.

"Is she...um—"

"Yes, she is the only human with whom the experiment worked. Well...the only one left with it active. Many humans had it, but it was deactivated because like you said, it never worked. But she is the exception, and this procedure needs to work."

Frankie tried to say a word, but her mouth would not move, not even a sound made it out. She found out that also moving her eyeballs was a great effort, and demanded a significant amount of concentration, and then she saw a translucent mask coming from afar, to then be in contact with her skin.

"It's okay Frankie, all will be fine.

# VEDI, VINI, VICI

A week had passed since the procedure, but it had only been two hours since Frankie was able to open her eyes, and move her arms. Dr. Gillman would come by her side every five minutes or so to check on her reflexes, and basic health. She would flash a light in her eyes, prick the tip of her fingers,
and toes.

"Ouch!"

"Finally." Dr. Gillman sighed with great relief when Frankie noticed her brow muscle lifting as she closed her eyes, "Captain, Miss.

Stein is awake, and responding."

"I'm on my way."

Frankie looked around her, and saw that outside the perimeter of her bed, and both columns on each side, the medical facility was brightly lit. Where she was, it had a dark blue light with only faint pink beams to show specific operating tools behind her. She wondered how that was possible but was grateful not to be in bright light as she didn't think her eyes could adjust yet—Frankie always had a better sight in the dark, medical tests from her teenage years mentioning she had high levels of vitamin A in her system, resulting in photonic-sensitivity. Frankie could remember most of what happened before the procedure. She could even recall her outburst in front of the Captain through the monitor screen. King, and Alaska had been by her side before, now Frankie suspected they were on duty. Her memory was clearly recovering, but she couldn't remember everything just yet.

"Now that I know you can understand me, Frankie. I can let you know that you are improving just fine, and at a faster rate than I thought you would."

Dr. Gillman's voice was different than what she remembered before the operation, it was soft, and peaceful. She even caressed her cheek with the back of her fingers covered in osteoderm like bony plates, and a smile flourished on her smooth face. Frankie felt strong, and as if her head was lighter, yet, fuller.

"I feel different."

"Yes, it's the Grey gene, or at least that is what I believe is causing this rate of change. It is now fully activated, streaming along your blood cells. It is adapting to your genetics quite fast. It started by regenerating your organs, then your brain. I kept a full report of your recovery and witnessed changes in specific areas such as muscle tissues, ligaments, and tendons. Your nervous system is more acute and responsive, making your senses keener than regular humans of any century. You are evolved."

Regenerate, evolved? Frankie looked at herself, and around her. She noticed that colors seem more vibrant than before, and she could almost hear what sounded like white noise in the background.

"Am I a metahuman now?"

Dr. Gillman chuckled, "Sort of, but I'd say more like a human, version 2.0."

The simple thought of having what could be viewed as superpowers had Frankie thinking about her past until she realized, "I remember things." She saw in her mind memories as if it happened moments ago, the first time she met Alaska. She was at the door of her house, dressed like any other woman her age, and her hieroglyphs tattoos were covered by her ghostly white skin tone. Behind her was the tall, and slim Dr. Gillman, but she looked like an athletic African American woman, "We were all wearing holographic projectors to have us look like humans of your century."

Fast forwarding to more recent events...

# A.D WAYNE

0500 Hours, 14th of October 2510
(Gregorian calendar,)
Milky Way Galaxy, Leo Constellation,
*Slicer*, Command Room.

"*Slicer* will soon need repairs. The plasma core needs to be attended, and the FTL engine requires more fuel. For that to happen, we need to stop at the next space station. I need
more blubber."

Alaska's voice might have been small, and soft, but when she wanted attention, she would place both her hands on the conference table. She looked straight in the eyes of the Captain unafraid to let him know the status of his ship.

"Let's go to the 12th century Earth, and extract what we need from a whale without hurting it in any way like we always do, and—"

"Pardon me Sir, but you don't understand, the FTL engine is shot, and if that won't work, neither will the Temporal motor. *Slicer* is stuck here in Rake Space just as I predicted six months ago."

Alaska looked around the room with a grave look on her face. Her eyes were wide open, and her lips tightly shut. She firmly said, her body ready to leave, but her head fixed on the senior crew, "If there's a next time, maybe you'll listen to your Chief Engineer, instead of thinking you understand this so-called, *Slicer* ship."

She turned on her heels, and walked out of the room in her navy-blue cargo pants, multitasking black belt, and a fitted grey t-shirt. Her goggles held her black graduated bob haircut back away from her face, showing her well defined light blue hieroglyphs tattoos on her face.

"We used all reserved fuel for that stupid last jump. Now we're stuck in Rake Space! We'll be lucky to survive the week if I don't repair the shields."

Her mumblings caught Frankie's attention, and so she ignored the Captain, and ran to her best friend walking across the bridge. Both hands in a fist, Frankie followed her to the corridor where she asked how they would get away from dangerous territories.

"We don't. We're screwed! It's over, Frankie!" Alaska replied with her hands up in the air as she took a deep breath, "There's nothing my team, and I can do this time. The Captain pushed our repairs for too long. *Slicer* cannot survive another jump, another attack, or another long-lasting pursuit." The short engineer genius took a deep breath, "Our best chance at survival would be the escape pods, and aiming for the closest 'out of danger' planet in this sector. There, we could start digging tunnels, and live like meerkats so as not to be detected by neither Rakes nor the Dome's Agents."

"Even that has..." Frankie calculated mimicking short gestures of equations in the air, "...about 14% of success."

"That sounds about right, Einstein."

As they both crossed over to the mess hall, Alaska stopped to get something to eat before heading back toward engineering at the back of the ship in the lower levels. Alaska confessed a while ago loving having to walk across what became the 'rotary meat plow corridor' separating Engineering from the rest of the ship due to its biohazard, radioactivity, and volatile mechanic levels. The rotary mechanism, exposed to the people crossing the corridor, made them quite uncomfortable due to its horrifying look as if ready to plow the engineers alive.

"You still love that meat plow corridor?"

"You bet, I do! It's what keeps the ship's magnetic field at normal levels, so us engineers don't have to suffer from dementia, nausea, or vertigo. That corridor saves us from insanity. So, what, if it needs a monthly organic sacrifice!" Alaska finished on a joke.

She grabs herself a green pear, and pasta salad with a large bottle of water, and went to sit down by Frankie who grabbed a peanut butter sandwich, and lactose-free chocolate milk. "Our Captain is focused on the mission, but he doesn't understand that the mission can only last as long as *Slicer* is capable of sustaining us. She's not. She's coughing plasma left and right, and the engine is spitting goo." Alaska lifted her eyes to meet Frankie's, and points her fork at her, "*Slicer*'s been running for six years non-stop, and this ship's not young anymore." Alaska leaned in, "This ship is not what it appears to be, Frank. I know because I'm the one running its core. I told the Captain she needed a rest, but does he listen to me? No."

"Have you told the Captain about the ship not being what it's supposed to be?"

"No, because I think he knows what the ship is."

Alaska's head shook wildly as she demonstrated her anger through her hand gestures, exaggerated with each word coming out of her mouth, "I'm just a human! I know nothing about space-time travel! I'm human! I'm stupid, and irrelevant to the survival of the universe! I'm just a backward species from a backward world!" She mumbled some more words between her teeth, and added, "Stupid, Captain, he's only like a quarter Walrian. As far as I'm concerned, he's more human than I am!"

Frankie sat there, and listened to the closest friend she had ever had in her entire life. Alaska, with her friendly green eyes rounded like a doll, her porcelain skin, and her small little mouth. She had the biggest heart in that part of the galaxy, and the kindest personality she had ever encountered.

"I think you would agree with me." Frankie looked at her best friend but refused to say a word, as she wanted her to vent as much as she could. "Your Grey gene knows what's up." The Chief Engineer pricked a piece of pear, and brought it to her mouth. She chewed on it, and said, "If only I knew more about what this ship is. I'm telling you Frankie; this ship is more than meets the eye."

People were walking around the mess hall, coming, and going. Frankie could tell Alaska wanted to be in her quarters, far away from every alien on the ship that made her feel inferior to others her rank. Then, a medium height dark grey-skinned man approached Alaska from behind, and with his webbed fingers hid her eyes. "How's my human princess?" he whispered as he bent over before sitting by her side. "She's fed up with everything." Alaska smiles, but the worry has yet to leave her eyes.

Frankie decided to leave the couple alone, and wished Alaska a good day before moving with her sandwich hanging from her mouth. She held her drink, and decided it was time for her to walk back to her quarters. She had a lot to think about, the ship and its relation to Caldwell. She knew something was wrong with the ship. She had known it from the moment she came into contact with it.

"You're hungry today." The voice was grave. Frankie felt a tingling of her skin when she bumped into a tall, and broad body. "Frankie, I need you to come with me. We are going on a very important mission. King, and Wolf are waiting."

"THE SHIP WAS SUPPOSED to be empty, no survivors. My scanning officer detected the molecules needed for *Slicer* to be repaired, and some other spare parts we would need to get out of Rake Space." The silence felt cold, and somewhat heavy on Frankie's shoulders, "I did not anticipate PBU devices to be available to the Rakes. We needed Wolf for his linguistic assimilation capability. King was our guns, and while I know Rake ships by heart…"

PBU, Frankie remembered it meant Portable Beaming Units—meaning they were 'a' to 'b' transporting devices. Then, she wondered why she had been part of the mission, she was still recovering and regenerating her memory. She tried to remember the Captain's orders, now that she could feel the same emotion she had always felt in his presence, the desire to know more about him.

"Captain, why was I present to recover blubber units for the ship? It doesn't make any sense to me."

"Your martial art skills are undeniably more efficient than anyone else's aboard my ship. Your presence on *Slicer* has been crucial since the beginning."

That was no answer. Frankie was not military, and she was from the less advanced century on the ship. What Captain Caldwell wanted, she figured, was the Grey gene to make her stronger and more dominant than anyone else around him, so that she could become his personal 'SEAL' officer. Frankie's eyes were now blurred by the thought of Caldwell being exactly what King had told her he was since the beginning, a selfish son of a bitch.

"Tell me I'm wrong, please…after all we have shared, please tell me I'm wrong."

"You are. I ordered Dr. Gillman to activate your Grey gene so that you could protect your mind from anyone attempting to steal or replicate what was given to you. This was the second attempt the Dome made! Who knows how many more procedures they would have in store, if you're ever caught again." Caldwell had to be telling the truth because she remembered Dr. Gillman mentioning that she could create an organic shield around her brain.

"I needed you on my ship to protect you, but you quickly became useful to *Slicer* in many other ways. Your knowledge of ancient human history, mixed with your acute sense of deduction has proven to be indispensable to us."

Frankie listened to Captain Caldwell's voice, low, and masterful, with a soft smoke that had her swear sometimes he was from Celtic descent, more specifically from Ireland. It was in his way of pronouncing certain words that she could hear the enthralling color of phonetics. He stood tall, and straight at the end of her bed, looked her in the eyes, and leaving her weak as he imposed respect wherever he was. "You are the only key we have to unlock the Grey's mysterious technology before the Dome regains power, and salvages it for themselves before we can retrieve it." She closed her eyes. "You translated half their instructions already. Without you, *Slicer* would be nothing."

Frankie remembered, "You needed someone from the twenty-first century, because all ancient knowledge of Earth was lost in the final war. Going back and forth in time, had you and the Dome changing Earth's history in many dimensions. You needed someone that would be too dumb to take over *Slicer*, but smart enough to translate things for you. I was a monkey, no, actually worse than that. I was a rented mule...wasn't I?"

The Captain slowly closed his eyes as his head leaned forward, and his breathing was louder as he raised his gaze again. "You've proven us all wrong. Don't you remember? You've put us all, including me, back in our place quite a few times over these past four years." He stepped forward, grabbed on to the bar at the foot of the bed, and said, "You said it yourself eighteen months ago. Your face was covered in mechanic oil, blood, and flesh was torn on your knuckles. Your hair was falling down from your bun as you stomped onto my bridge, and stopped before my chair. You threw the electronic tablet at my feet. I looked down for a second before meeting your dark hazel green eyes. The tablet contained important encrypted codes from the Greys' logs that a Rake pirate ship had stolen from another LSS vessel belonging to the planet Liberty that retreated during the attack. We needed it. Our orders were to retrieve that tablet at all costs." He took a deep breath, moved his eyes around, and looked back at her feet, "Your skin seemed like it went through a cloud of smoke, glimmering in the light of my bridge showing your sweat, blood, and stains. You looked into my eyes without a fear, and a deep frown I remember. Your black tank top was torn on the side but not your grey one underneath. You had no weapons, except those you had stolen from the Rakes. You turned off your optical emitter that transmitted a live video of your actions. I will never forget the tone of your voice, passionate, and strong, 'I came, I saw, I conquered.' We could feel the heaviness of the silence in the room when you added, 'Julius Caesar. Look him up.'"

Frankie was lost in his words as she relived the memory with Captain Caldwell who added, "We all looked at you as you wiped the blood dripping from your nose with your arm, you made us fear humans the moment you said, 'Because humans are conquerors, not explorers. I'll help you end the Rakes. The human way.' You were about to step off of my bridge, when I stood up to look at you the moment you added,

'Sneak peek at human history: when our European ancestors wanted to conquer lands, and countries, the Roman General Scipio Aemilianus Africanus plowed over, and strewed the village of Carthage with salt after defeating it in the Third Punic War, and enslaved the survivors. Let's take the idea, and apply it to your twenty-sixth-century shit war.' There was nothing more I could have asked of you. That's why you are my best asset, and the one I hold most dear."

Frankie didn't know if the anger she spoke that day was a good reflection on what humanity had been. But in her head, she knew human history was written in blood. She studied it, read it, and if one species knew how to exterminate another, humans were the right choice, as sad as it was. Maybe some part of human history would be better left unspoken, but through it all, it made Frankie's species true survivors. When she looked up into the eyes of the Captain, he put his hand forward and said, "Will you not hold to your words, Commander Stein?" She took his hand, and as they shook she said, "I will, Captain Caldwell

# THE HUMAN KNOCK-OUT

The Alliance gave Captain Caldwell carte blanche as to who would constitute his main crew onboard *Slicer*. When Frankie stepped on board, never would Captain Caldwell have thought about putting her among his most trusted crew members. Yet, once she proved herself to him over and over, he made her an Unofficial Liberty Officer. When his actions were doubted by the Liberty Council a few months after Frankie joined the away missions' team, he had Frankie stand by his side in his bridge office.

Captain Caldwell displayed all the artifacts she had retrieved, the number of Rakes she had killed, and how many of his crewmen she saved. "How many times did she, and I have to save your sorry Walrians asses because you didn't have the balls to do it?" Caldwell had said. His head might have been low, but his brows were raised to demonstrate that he was ready for any type of confrontation. He looked straight into the holographic image of the Alliance Council's highest member. "That's what I thought." He said as all members stayed silent. "You're fucking welcome," he then ended the transmission.

Ever since that day, Frankie knew her emotions toward him would be harder to dissimulate. She might have heard a thousand times over that Captain Caldwell was not to be trusted, because of his murky past, and because he was thought to have some Walrian DNA. *"The Walrians are a peaceful race. Those aliens show up to save people, and help them in their quest to join space missions. The thing is, because they help almost every alien race around, they think they are entitled to belittle others. Especially humans. I won't stand for that. So, I like to remind them that if every punch is a knock-out to them, that they should leave real missions to humans because we're made to take hits better than anyone. You proved it."*

Yet that morning, those words of comfort surfacing in her head from a not so distant memory wasn't enough. She was now the Captain's right-hand man, and first in command after him. She remembered how near he stood when admitting he had never felt closer to anyone else on his ship since she walked into his life. It didn't matter how deeply touched she felt, all that she recalled was the sensation of an uneasy chill going up her spine to the back of her neck, and spreading through her brain. That morning, she looked up in the mirror of the locker room where she stood after taking her shower. She wore a dark grey sports bra, and tight boy short underwear. She was untangling her midnight blue-black hair, which had been growing ever since she was brought onboard *Slicer*. She then twisted it, and pinned it to her head, ready in case of an unexpected mission. Frankie had both her hands resting on the counter. Her head down, she closed her eyes, and took a minute to forget about all that happened to her in the past few years, and tried to regain confidence in herself.

Despite fighting certain aspects of her mental health, Frankie had been able to function as one of the crew. She even climbed up the ladder quite fast in rank, despite never having been part of any military - Earth or otherwise. She based her knowledge and decisions on video games, and the space fiction series she had watched. After more than four years, she now knew how the routine worked, and picked up on the rhythm of the Alliance and Liberty military defenses. But it all felt natural to her. When she finally walked out of the locker room, she wore a black long sleeve shirt, and fitted cargo pants. She walked toward the mess hall where she met Wolf on his way to have breakfast.

"Commander Stein!" He said with a bright smile when Frankie stopped him, "Please, don't ever call me that." Her friend naturally wondered if Frankie could hear the murmur of the bridge crewmembers. The gossip spread around the ship like fake news on TV. As they passed by very slowly, Frankie facing Wolf felt the other crew members move, and understood them clearly with her acute sense of hearing. "How many times do you think she fucked Caldwell to get that promotion?" While some others said, "Apparently it still works when you're a human girl to get to the top by standing on your knees." The last one, "Human women, they are the trash of the Orion Quadrant."

Frankie raised her arm, and shoved a hard elbow to the back of the female Reptilian's head. Frankie then grabbed her by the neck, and propelled her violently against the wall. She then used her momentum to give a hard hit to the solar plexus of the Zelron male with the base of her palm, and he knocked himself out on the wall. Frankie looked at the other female alien, giving her enough time to think Frankie wouldn't do anything. The moment she lowered her guard she grabbed her by the back of the neck, and forcefully raised her knee. The contact between her forehead, and the rotula was heard as a hollow echo. Everyone stopped, and some joined from the mess hall to stand with the others watching.

"I am your superior officer, Commander Stein," Frankie said with a loud, and proud voice before all crew members, stupefied, and in shock. With a grave dictatorial look on her face, never had Frankie broke a sweat, she added, "You will address me as such, and with respect." She looked around, "Humans know war. Women of Earth know the meaning of losing their freedom, being shamed, and degraded, raped, and abused." Everyone stared at her with eyes wide opened as she paced around the corridor staring down at all of them who had dared talk behind her back, "I know what it's like to be rejected, judged, backstabbed, and called names. I even know what it is to have rumors spread about me without a chance to defend myself." She looked down at the floor where the girl she knocked on the forehead laid, and said with a voice burning with pride of the woman she had become, "Human women are not the trash of the Orion Quadrant, they are the pillars of your future because without us there is no before or after. Read your history appropriately before you decide to attack one with it."

Frankie needed no Captain to back her up. She stood tall and proud because she knew the choice was made based on her skills, and not at how low she would go to get a promotion she didn't even desire in the first place. Frankie looked at everyone, and with a robust superlative voice she said, "Dismissed!" She stared at the crew present who witnessed her specific skills at taking down three of the security team, trained by the Alliance military like they were simple cadets.

"You still stand by your statement that you had no military training?" Wolf asked in awe looking at his close friend who kept her facial expression strict, cold, and authoritarian until all of them walked in the direction they were supposed to attend. When alone, Frankie released a strong exhale, and said, "All I had was a SEAL as an ex, hours of playing sci-fi warfare video games, and Trek binge watching under my belt. Oh, and not to mention a creed teaching me history." Noticing the confusion on Wolf's face, she explained, "It doesn't matter the century, the species or the place in time. Sexism and racism always seem to find a way to get in. Women have to work double for the respect they deserve regardless of their skills. Also, I guess the galaxy doesn't give a shit about the century we're in either, hatred seems to still be up to date."

Wolf approved after confessing to being judged as well for being an Olymnu. He used to be a meteorologist before convincingly being asked to join the crew of Caldwell. His species had a rapid way of assimilating not only languages, but reading people, and their body language, it had *Slicer* stop by his planet. "My planet is Olympe, we're Olymnus, and apparently, according to their analysts, I was an Olymnu 2.0. I am the next step in the evolution of my people. My senses are more acute, and not only do I assimilate languages, and read people, but I can also read short moments in their minds as well as camouflage myself like an Earth chameleon." Frankie admitted still being curious about his genetics that permitted his skin to change at will. The Olymnu, similar in look as a Reptilian, such as Dr. Gillman, often had Frankie laughing, and she enjoyed his company. When stepping into the mess hall, all present stood up. Frankie didn't know how to react. Wolf leaned over, "It's genuine." Frankie bowed, and said, "At ease. I am not your Captain." All went back to their previous activities, and Frankie suddenly felt a knot in her middle. She walked out of the mess hall, Wolf by her side, "Let's go see Dr. Gillman. You're having another anxiety attack."

They both ran to the medical deck, and once inside, Wolf stated, "All who don't need immediate medical attention, leave. Commander Stein requires privacy, now!" Those in for a simple check-up from the nurses, and doctors left. Dr. Gillman walked over to Frankie who kept her head low, so as not to show herself on the verge of crying without reason. "Safescreen!" Wolf firmly said with his friendly voice. Despite trying to sound rigid, it sadly still came out playful. A transparent dome appeared around Dr. Gillman, Wolf, and Frankie who wouldn't let go of her friend's hand as he held her in his arms. "You can lift up your head, Frankie. No one can see inside the safescreen."

Frankie released many tears. Dr. Gillman gave her one injection of what they called Buffer. "You'll carry them as of now on you. Each shot is good for twenty-four hours. You have six shots in each package I gave you. They fit in the hidden pocket of the official senior commanding officer cargo pants you'll get soon." Frankie noticed how often Gillman looked up at Wolf without a smile, she said, "Wolf won't say a word. He's the one who brought me here and felt my anxiety." Wolf swore secrecy, and said, "If it's of any meaning to you, Doctor, I am more pleased to know my Commander feels something, than a Captain who doesn't feel anything at all."

The knot began to untangle, and loosen. Frankie felt better, and started regaining her own confidence. Wolf mentioned that no one would ever know as long as she would keep up with her emotions. He suggested that the second she would feel doubt, to take one of the buffer shots. Dr. Gillman added patches in the package saying "Those are for emergencies. You can use no more than two a day. They are immediate relief without any side effects. So, no worries." By the tone of Dr. Gillman's voice, Frankie understood that it had to be kept a secret, that even in the century she was in, mental illnesses were still taboo. Despite Frankie's understanding of not wanting to have an unstable Captain at the head of a ship, if all medications were this useful, why hide it? "Not every species on board is acceptant of medications, especially when it comes to the brain. For many, if the emotions, and brains are affected, it means weaknesses." Then they all heard the powerful voice of the Captain.

"Commander Stein, Lieutenant Wolf report to the bridge."

Dr. Gillman looked down, "I've seen what trauma does to brave and courageous people. They come out of those battles beaten, afraid, and trying to understand what happened to them. You are more than what your anxiety tells you. Frankie, you are the warrior that we all see, and admire. Some might not see it yet, but in time, they will. I promise."

"Commander Stein?"

"Aye, Captain. We are both on our way."

The safescreen now down, Frankie thanked Gillman and walked out of the medical facility stronger and better. She took a second to hold her white gold cross in her hand chained to her neck. Somehow, it reminded her of the life she had before *Slicer*. When they got into the elevator, Wolf asked her what it represented. "It's an Earth faith, an old one...it might sound crazy to you, but despite being here among the stars in another time among aliens, this little cross holds me steady and reminds me of where I come from." Wolf nodded, but then asked what the cross itself represented, "A human invention that brought nothing but shame in human history. If there was one torture device that should've never seen the light of day because of its horrifying everlasting agony, this here is the winner. It held the body of one man who taught nothing but love, and acceptance. Some of us wear it in reminiscence of what he stood for." Wolf asked why humans put what seemed to have been a kind and honorable man to death. "Because we are conquerors, not explorers or lovers."

"Well, we might win this war after all," Wolf said with a smile.

The bridge was situated in a very secure placement of the ship. Centered below upper decks, it was heavily protected by thick anti-bombing walls made of an alien material Frankie had never heard about. She knew the primary monitor was not a window, but literally a screen that permitted the crew to see what was in front of them. It projected live images of what space looked like around them, which mostly was entirely black with some debris floating by from time to time, and a distant sun. Often, the monitor would display zooming images when scans would detect movement or light. That usually meant "Code Hades," which meant a battle might take place.

"Stein, Wolf. The scanners detected another Rake ship, a quarter of a light year from here. The Decoder can achieve that distance assuming the Rakes' ship Decoder is working. Commander King is already working on it remotely, and will then accompany you as usual."

Captain Caldwell showed them on the main screen the carcass of the ship. "I need you both to get to the engineering room, and get their plasma container, blubber supply, and anything else on the list Alaska shared on your arm bracers." Then he looked at Frankie, "You, Stein. I need you to get to the leader's quarters, and copy his logs. We need to know what the Rakes are planning with the Dome. You are the only one capable of reading ancient Earth languages. There might be something we need."

Frankie nodded, then left the bridge accompanied by Wolf, and King. As they walked to the weapon's locker, she wondered if she was being armed this time. However, King reminded her that somehow the Captain might have other obscure reasons for stopping her from wearing the highly sophisticated weaponry. "No weapon, no me on this mission. Tell the Captain I'll be in the lab decoding the Grey's artifacts." Frankie turned on her heels, and was about to walk out the door when King grabbed her hand gently. The man was about six feet tall, a head taller than her. His eyes were wolf shaped, and had long eyelashes, while the dark color of the night had her hypnotized when crossing his nightly gaze, his hair, just as dark, was thick, and silky straight, braided behind his head while the tone of his flesh reminded her of gold.

"Here, these are—"

"Tomahawks. Those are old, almost dating back to the Revolutionary War."

"Yes. You know about—?"

"I'm human too, remember?"

King took off his military Alliance shirt, turned around, and lifted his black tee. Frankie could see his muscular, and large imposing back. She saw the tattoo of a Native American eagle on his shoulder blades. It reminded her that First Nations had made it to the future. King represented a part of her family's history, as her mother shared the blood of the Mohawk people.

"I never asked, what is your people?" She wondered if Mohawks actually survived all the wars and centuries. After all, First Nations in the twenty-first century alone were not a great percentage of the Earth's population.

"I am part of the Sioux." He had a smile that always had Frankie feel her cheeks warming up, "I noticed you brought a painting of a Sioux male you made." Frankie laughed, "Don't think I don't know what you're doing! Back off, Romeo."

He had a small smile in the corner of his mouth, full lips, and perfectly hairless skin making his jawline appear squarer than it was. He then turned to the locker on his right, grabbed a knife holster, and asked, "Have you ever worn one of those?" Frankie nodded, and he said while kneeling in front of her, "Well, I'm going to place it on you anyways. First you attach the holster to your belt."

Frankie observed him tying the holster around her waist. He wrapped it around her thigh, his touch might have been mechanical at first, but he slowed down. His brows lowered in the centered when he suddenly looked up, "You're all set." He smiled while both his hands rested on her hips, and Frankie barely found the strength to say, "Thank you." She knew King had feelings for her, and while she found him attractive, it stopped at his kindness for her. Her heart, somehow, belonged to the man sitting in the commanding chair.

Wolf was ready to leave but said that he didn't wish to be a third wheel, "I can come back later when Alaska shouts that she needs more blubber." King smiled, and chuckled, "Because I would have my first time with Frank in the locker room! How sexy of me." Frankie stopped on her march, and wished she hadn't heard him because his friendship meant more to her than anything else. Caldwell was still on her mind. She acted as if she heard nothing between King and Wolf and followed them outside the room.

The salvaging team walked toward the Decoder that was situated three hundred meters away from the weapon room. When walking by the entrance, a scanner detected their weaponry, and marked it on their mission report automatically. When Frankie walked in, the guard mentioned that she was not allowed weaponry. King made it clear when he grabbed the guard by the collar, and pulled him toward his chest off the ground, "Do you wish for me to teleport you on that ship without any weapons, Cadet? What if there are a few Rakes that are left, want me to teleport you there, scumbag?" He shook the male guard as hard as he could, and growled, "Answer me!" With his rough voice, as if he always had a constant wolf-like snarl, he waited for the answer that the guard shook his head, "No, Sir." He then quickly let him down with the least care, "Well she's already faced Rakes, enough times without any weapons thanks to our superiors. I thought that proved her mental strength enough."

The guard said he would have to contact the Captain or the Admiral. King pushed the man away from the controls, and wrote himself, "Permission given by Lieutenant Commander Nakamo King, Code 106658. Permission Level five Gamma 2." He then turned his head to the guard, "Here, and if the Captain says anything, tell him he'll have to take it up with me."

Frankie wanted to stop her friend, but they both shared the same status at that moment, and even though it rarely affected her judgment, this time it meant something for her. He defended her right to protect herself. She had a hard time believing it was by Caldwell's doing that she wasn't allowed to have weaponry. However, at this moment, she had no time to solve that mystery. Yet, she couldn't shake her doubts about Caldwell, something in her gut was telling her that he was not the threat. Frankie could still hear King's mumblings while grinding his teeth, "Motherfucking Alliance can kiss my fucking ass. Stupid cocksucking Caldwell, three-quarter human my ass."

Frankie watched him walking up the stairs to the circled pedestal illuminated by a hundred arctic white light bulbs. Above their heads was the same circle of light, and then King said, "Get us out of here, now Cadet." He softly moved in front of Frankie as if to protect her if something would happen when decoded onboard the Rakes' ship. As the vibration quickened between the pulses, circles of light were transferred from the bottom receiver to the top, and slowly, they disappeared only to reappear in the teleportal room onboard the Rakes' ship. When the light faded, and the vibration pulses disappeared, the two were placed to shoot while Frankie was ready to throw a tomahawk, King asked, "Is everyone okay?" The room was empty, and showed the aftermath of some sort of internal explosion. "Aye." Frankie, and Wolf replied in a whisper as they moved away from the platform.

The ship was a wreck, wires were hanging from the ceiling some still emitting sparks, the artificial gravity on, and oxygen level still going. The away team slowly left the Decoder room, and worked themselves into the corridor. Wolf activated the holographic map from an emitter on his arm bracer, and guided them to the first junction. One-way led to the engine room while the other would bring them to the main bridge.

"I will cover Commander Stein, while you go to salvage what can be used on *Slicer*. We meet at the rendezvous point in an hour."

"Aye. Good luck, Commanders!"

The walls of the Rakes' ship were covered in different rectangle sizes of a greyish tone with a hint of red with the texture of boiled leather grafted on the framing of each metallic panel inspired fright in Frankie. Numerous beams of wood shaped like spears were coming out of the grid floors, at almost every meter, and clearly held something. But the emergency lights going on and off like the life support system was about to let go, made it very hard for anyone to see clearly.

Frankie refused to think about the inside of the ship, as it had provoked night terrors the first time she set foot in a Rakes' vessel. It took her months of treatment by Dr. Gillman to calm those down. Still to this day, she could wake up in the middle of the night sweating and screaming.

The air in the ship was stagnant, the humidity level higher than it should've been. When pressure was released from the ceiling, a strong smell of feces would hit both Frankie, and King. It was then followed by an intense mix of rotten eggs, musty mothballs, and fermenting cabbage. Such a smell does not erase itself from anyone's mind who had to cross the path of what was known as a Legion Ship. Navigating through the corridor, slowly brought her, and King to the main bridge. She tried to fix an imaginary point at the end of their path as he told her in the past to try, and ignore the side walls. The light was getting brighter and the smell reminded her that it could quickly be coming from her if one Rake was still alive.

"Sir? The main support system is on and running well." Wolf mentioned to Frankie as she was higher in rank than King, even though he was leading the mission as the Tactical Officer specialized in terrain missions. "Good job, Wolf."

The lights were bright. King, and Frankie were standing on the bridge where the smell seemed stronger than on the rest of the ship. When looking around, Frankie recognized the decorations of impaled heads at the end of each spear, intestines hooked to the ceiling like festive garlands, and back skin of aliens and humans grafted to the walls like a tapestry. Bones attached to each commanding post like altars had Frankie remembering the eyeballs that were used as necklaces, with teeth as decorations around belts of the Rakes that seemed to have abandoned the ship.

"The ship is empty, Frankie. You have nothing to worry about. I doubled checked, and there are no life signs onboard." His voice might have been low, comforting, and followed with a kind rub on her denuded shoulders, but Frankie knew better when she answered with moisture in her eyes, "That's what you said last time."

# LAST TIME AGAIN

Rumbling was heard. Chants of metal against metal grids starting from afar coming nearer with each massive step. Like an army, walking in harmony, with a baritone note that was sung.

King ran to the commanding seat, and had the doors locked using an emergency setting that Wolf had been able to translate a few Legion warships ago with the unique linguistic skills that he adapted for each away mission team. Frankie wore the cybernetic contact lenses that contained various vital information, including Wolf's translation of the Rake's language. Those contact lenses were not just applied on the main crew's eyeballs but plugged to their ocular nerves connected to their brain's network. This system made each member temporary Cyborgs. The first time Frankie put them on, she remembered the sting, and the pressure it caused until the robotic arm attached itself to her nervous system. After that, Frankie decided not to remove the cybernetic lenses. Instead, she only updated the information by injections, like most people on board the *Slicer* that were chosen for missions.

Feeling trapped, Frankie looked at King entering a rotating segment of codes to keep the doors locked to the bridge. He then ensured that the bridge itself was now separated from the rest of the ship to protect Frankie at all costs. She knew. It had been as such since the beginning of her missions with King, and Wolf. The reason for King to cut off the bridge from the rest of the starship was to make sure life support wouldn't be deleted. Hence, Frankie was able to accomplish what she was sent to do: hack the Rake's computer system, and copy the Captain's logs, find anything related to the Greys, load it, and bring it back to *Slicer*.

Frankie was the only one capable of recognizing the hieroglyphic language left by the Greys. Even Wolf wasn't capable of translating it or seeing any differences between the Rakes' tricked and false hieroglyphs that had sent the *Slicer* on false chases before Frankie joined the crew. Wolf was first thought capable of such a task, due to his evolving DNA, but sadly, the Rakes had been more effective at eluding the Olymnu. So, Frankie was then seen as the most valuable asset. Wolf had proven to be indispensable himself, as he was capable of now faking his way into the Rakes' logs, and to mess up orders, and read into their top-secret missions. That was how he discovered they were parallelly working with the Dome. It had Captain Caldwell wondering about the reason why, but so far, Wolf hadn't found the root of their relationship.

At that moment, Frankie was immobile before the door banged from the outside. "What are you doing, Frankie? Get the info so we can get out of here!" She might have heard King, but Frankie's eyes were stuck on the door, her body numb, she whispered, "That's what you said last time, and the time before that, and the time before that." Then she heard, "Frankie!" Without her, the mission had no purpose. Without her help, they might die. King contacted Wolf and asked if he was being attacked by the Rakes.

"Not yet, but it won't be long."

"Okay, use the ventilation system to crawl back to the Decoder room, and transport off the ship." King reminded Wolf to wait for him to give him the green light, so he could lock the ventilation system from the bridge to stop any Rakes from grinding them to human meat. "Now!"

Hefty, echoing, ranging banging on the door by a cacophony of fists, leaving the walls almost shaken by their powerful grip, had Frankie caught in a loop. Memories surfacing of her first time fighting the Rakes. Sure, she mastered Keysi, and knew Krav Maga, but it was their eyes... glowing like beasts, as if peering into her soul, and sucking it from her very mind. Then, there was so much blood, she might have never drawn weapons first, but she had drawn the first blood.

"Frankie!" King yelled.

"So much blood." Moisture slowly taking over her eyes, she mumbled words almost made-up to anyone who would've heard them spoken aloud, "Nothing begins. Nothing ends." She felt a sting on her arm. She looked down, and saw King holding the plastic tip of a syringe between his teeth. The buffer. Suddenly, she swallowed up her tears. Looked around and found the science station on the bridge. She logged into the computer and looked through files. She ordered the contact lenses with a thought to look for one word, "Gamma" written in the Rakes' language.

The constant heavy banging on the bridge's doors now had no effect on Frankie, but had her cringing nonetheless as she tried to stay focused on the task at hand. She then started to hear nails on the metal, scratching the doors, and knew she had to work faster. Thanks to her years of studies in computer programming, and web design, she was capable of typing at an almost inhuman rate of a hundred and five words per minute. She looked at the monitor, and kept scrolling, and then found the word. A hurried voice, as he was trying to set up a defence system, King asked with a very deep husk in his voice, "What are you doing?"

"What I was sent to do." She said with a stern monotone voice.

She opened the encrypted file by bypassing the security system attached to it, and when it finally began downloading, she loaded the information by placing a small, ten centimeters by five centimeters translucent electronic tablet over the monitor.

"If you knew where the folder was kept, why not just load the whole thing, and be done with it?"

"You want to carry a virus on board *Slicer*, and have our life support system shut down? The virus was protecting the folder from thieves. I had to first get rid of the virus, and then find the mother folder to load it without harm."

"They've never done that before!"

"No, they're adapting to our tactics, anticipating our every move. Theyare learning."

Frankie knew it was just a matter of time before they would now tear down the doors to the bridge. Then, it hit her. Somehow, someone had to be smarter than the Rakes to have thought of a virus, and orchestrate each attack, starting with the first time they had invaded their supposedly abandoned ship. At the command station, King was trying to type something, when she heard her name in a panic.

"Frankie, I need your help. I need you to—"

"Let them come." She answered calmly in a low voice, placing herself ready to attack, holding both King's tomahawks in her hands.

Pale greyish hands, with long bony fingers with claws made their way through the crevice where the two doors met, and pushed against the flaps to open. "Frankie..." King said again, looking toward her. She saw him from her peripheral vision, but her eyes were still fixed on the opening of the doors.

"I need to see him."

"You need to see whom?"

The doors opened, and King took out his plasma gun. Frankie jumped at the twelve Rakes she counted coming in, and stabbed both blades through two of the Rakes' under jaws, and slid them out while kicking one in the front to use him like a propeller to land on two others, and slashed their throats.

"Frankie!" King shouted as she answered, "The flamethrower, now!" She stood outside the bridge, and by killing four Rakes right when the doors were barely opened, the rest were still off the deck as she fought them off. Nine to go. Frankie heard the flamethrower, and ducked instantly. It set more than half of them on fire while spreading to the others. The doors closed just in time to protect King from a risk of backfire, and so she ran to a section at the starboard of the ship. Frankie remembered from the blueprints taken from the Legion that there was a section that seemed apart from the rest of the construction, and found a long corridor leading to a dark black door. She walked toward it, and saw a mechanism rolling counter-clockwise. She stepped away.

The odor of the place was still invading her nose, heads, and entrails were displayed as the door opened slowly. Every part of her was begging for her to run away, while something deep inside her mind said, "Do not be afraid." Frankie didn't know what she would see. All she was aware of, was her instinct to go toward the door, and face whatever would be inside. Frankie covered her mouth, and nose as the pressurized door panels released a smell of rotten meat. She wished she would have worn a hoodie of some sort, but she knew the Rakes' ships were often warm, and humid. A tank top seemed to be the best way to go.

"Nice lion on your left arm." A deep, and grave, but clear voice said with an accent reminiscent of Ireland. "Does it mean anything to you?"

Frankie tried to see through the darkness of the room, as the doors now slid back into their different compartments. The room drowned in pitch black, and all Frankie could see was a silhouette standing against a faint white light from the window behind him on his left. She took a deep breath, and regretted it almost instantly. The smell should've made her nauseated, but, somehow, she worked her way through it.

"Well?"

She glanced at her arm. The drawing was of a famous fictional lion standing proudly among dark clouds, with colorful reflections from the sky covered her upper left arm. It turned the tattoo into a half sleeve. Its symbolism reminded her of a distant life that now seemed to have been only a dream.

"Yes." She answered, cautious as her right brow lowered, and she focused her attention on the silhouette.

"What does it mean?" Immobile, same tone as before, almost robotic.

"Why do you want to know?" Squinting, she heard steps coming toward her, she grabbed onto her weapons ready to fight. She saw his hand reaching in the low yellow light of the corridor where she stood. It was as if he ordered the Rakes to stop. It all fell silent. She listened to the belly of the ship, its heart, and soul. It was alive, and felt as if it went farther than it should have. Something had created the Rakes. The answer was hidden in the deepest corners of space. She felt it while staring at the silhouette.

"Come in." His body moved to the side of the door as if to let her know it was safe to step into the dark room. "Tell me more about those...skin drawings of yours." Still grave, his gaze fixed on her as his profile didn't show in the shadows against the faint light, "Are they memories of obstacles in your life?"

Frankie wanted to look behind her, and count the Rakes, but she feared that if she looked anywhere else, the silhouette would disappear. "What is your name?" She asked, her head lowering, her chin almost in contact with her chest. "General Ash Zachariah of the UUS otherwise known as the Underworld Universe Society, *Cerberus II*," the silhouette replied.

The name, so human-like that he quickly stated, "I translated it to fit your language." "Does ash to ash have meaning to you?" Her head tilted, stepping forward almost in reach of his hand. She was now curious, and hungry for more information about the General, as he was definitely more humanoid than other Rakes she had encountered. "Yes." Still in the darkness, she saw his hand reaching for the white gold cross her mother had given her for her twenty-ninth birthday, and said, "We even have the same faith you, and I." Frankie refused to believe that a species as cruel, and sadistic as the Rakes could believe in heaven, or anything for that matter.

Frankie turned around, and saw about twenty Rakes all trying to jump over one another to reach to her. However, they were stopped by the will of one silhouette hidden in the dark. Their pale ashen bodies, reminiscent of a cadaver with blue lines showing their veins crawled all over their skin. They were hairless, and their jaw, elongated at the bottom, showed their teeth ready for action. Their mouths, foaming saliva, dripped from between razor-sharp teeth. Making noises with their ghostly voices, and swallowing air with the back of their tongue touching their larynx, they sounded like disembodied creatures in a quest for the next meal.

Frankie looked back at the silhouette, "Come." Frankie walked in, and the door stayed open. He reminded her that none of them would touch her unless he ordered them to do so. The alien pointed at a picture on his desk next to the tall, wide window. Unable to see his face in detail, Frankie could see he had long chestnut hair, two strands on each side stopped on either side of his head below his eyes. One she could see, while the other hid in the dark, but the hair reflected the light from the nebula outside his window. She wasn't done looking at him. His eyes, the color of lavender carried a story, and she saw a prominent scar on the iris. His skin, the color of topaz, had him look entirely different than the Rakes outside his quarters. She asked, "What are you?" Despite him wanting her to look at the picture, he stepped forward. Frankie felt discomfort, and worried about her safety, so she tightened her grip on the tomahawks, and looked up.

The room was too dark, despite her eyesight used to obscure places. "Use the Grey gene of yours." How did he know? The previous encounters with their ships must have been spread around, but she wondered how it reached him. She figured cameras must have taken pictures of her, and so she focused on his appearance. She saw through the lack of light, a metallic guard, almost like a muzzle attached from the tip of his nose to his chin. It went around his neck, and she saw it tying at the side of his jaw on both sides below his ears. The skin somewhat darker, made Frankie guess it was bruised.

"I'm a Rake." He said, his voice clearly coming from the metallic device, clear, and organic. Frankie didn't want to believe him, but why would he lie? "Then who are the ones outside?" She asked, stepping away, and signaling with her head, "Rakes." Impossible. He looked manly, human, despite the color of his eyes as the other looked blind, entirely white with a wide scar covering half the left of his face.

"Look at the picture." He pointed to the desk, and she turned around. Looking over her shoulder twice before reaching the gold frame, she held it toward her before turning it over. The picture showed a sugar maple, and a girl with natural wavy dark auburn hair, hazel green eyes, leaning up against the tree. The young woman wore her favorite sci-fi fitted tank top, and jeans. She had on light makeup, and was wearing her nerdy delicate bronze glasses. Her smile showed the diastema between her two front teeth.

"That's..." she let go of the frame in horror. A second later she gasped, "How did you get that picture?" Frankie was horrified. He held an electronic tablet in his hand, and said, "All your answers are in here." Rakes were heard shouting outside, no words, only louder wraithlike sounds. Some were low, while others were a high pitch, but together they created a harmony worthy of hell. She looked toward the door, and saw King on his knees. Rakes were holding him down, while a taller, stronger one held King's head by his hair exposing his throat.

"Rakes start their feast by plunging their claws deep under the rib cage. Then they drink the blood coming out, while others tear the fingers off, and nibble on them like they were delicacies." Frankie might have been listening to the calm, and relaxed voice of the one named, Zachariah, but she moved toward King before feeling the overly firm grip of the General. "Nakamo!" She shouted, her voice cracking under the pressure of her terror seeing him in such a vulnerable position. A memory resurfaced, one forgotten from an earlier mission.

"After the fingers are gone, the ears are chewed down by the sharp teeth of the alphas of the group. The meal is then brought to a long table where the body is tied down by a leather rope made of previous inedible meat." Zachariah held on to Frankie, keeping her in place, both his hands closing on her arms as she stood powerless. Memories were surfacing from images that had been hidden in the darkest corners of her mind to protect her sanity which was slowly sailing away. "Humans are delicacies. They are our favorite meals. We savor each bite like it might be our last," he added with a smile in his voice as she heard a more nasal tone. "You should be flattered. Your level of iron is high enough to compensate for our deficiencies, and your low fat is perfect for our system. You taste...irresistible."

Frankie tried to free herself, but all she did was mumble words of a not so distant past, and previous missions she fought at King's side. "We try to take our time eating our meal, but we can't hold it back for too long, as humans are not resistant to pain like us. See, we like to eat them while they are alive. Their eyes are the last bit to be consumed."

Rakes were getting closer to his rib cage, while others were feasting their eyes on his hands, she shouted, "Don't you dare touch him!" Double-jointed, Frankie gave herself a shot to dislocate both her shoulders. Taken by surprise, Zachariah released her while she popped her arms back in place, and hooked his elbow putting him down on his knees. "Release Commander King."

One move of his own, as he was double-jointed as well, he released himself, and held the tablet up in his hand again. "The tablet holds all the secrets to your life, Caldwell, and answers to all of your questions, or King. You can't have both."

Without hesitating one microsecond, Frankie responded "King." The General held his hand up high, and the Rakes walked away from the Commander. He slowly got back on his feet, and a few drops of his blood fell to the floor. His bottom lip was cut, and he was bleeding onto his shirt. Frankie saw Zachariah nodding, and the Alpha Rake moved up both his hands, and quickly tore the Commander's shirt off his back. He gave a loud cry that sounded like a beast in the wild, deep, and growly. Rakes tried to jump on the shirt covered in blood, but the tall alpha was already walking away, the Rakes following him like pests.

Frankie knew Zachariah was surprised at her decision, but she said, "I will be back for the tablet." A glance, and Zachariah answered, "I know you will. If not by your own agenda, then by mine." As she was about to run to the Decoder device, she felt intense pressure, and all went black.

# FRAME OF REFERENCE

Two days had passed since the mission. Frankie was on the edge of her bed, holding her head in her hands as her elbows rested on her knees. She wore loose jogging pants, and a fitted tank top she used to wear to sleep. She hadn't left her quarters since the last mission. Commander King was under care in the medical bay. She spent hours trying to understand how she had made a mistake. Why did she leave King alone? She tried to figure out why she was driven to that place to meet Zachariah. Why she decided that it was a good thing. Never had she left a crewmate alone, despite being armed or believed that they were safe.

She walked to the window of her bedroom, both hands pressed against the two meters' thick reinforced glass material. She didn't know the compound of the glass, an alien recipe she figured, and stared at the darkness of space.

*You're not military, Frankie. You're just a programmer...okay, maybe a little more than that. But you're a damaged chick nonetheless.*

She fell down on her knees. Frankie was fighting tears, and a choking cry. The sound was high enough to awaken Jerome, her new meerkat. He came down from her bed to crawl on her back onto her shoulders. She felt him but was unable to move. The smell of sulfur, heads impaled, rumbling hefty steps, and ghostly commotions swallowing back their own eerie noise. Half breathing, half choking, their voices were ones of nightmares. Cries, and screams. Limbs twitching from nerves detached. She tried to save the two men when turning the corner of the corridor leading to the teleportal room, but she was too late.

# FRANKENSTEIN

Frankie saw the Rakes feeding off their bodies as the men screams were being overthrown by their cries. She wished she had a gun. She wanted one, but instead all she had were throwing blades! She grabbed two impaled heads, and tossed them away. She pulled the spears, and aimed for their heads, hoping to hit between their eyes. All she could do was hope they died, but she already run away to the second room where King was waiting for her, and the tablet with the information she had to gather from the Greys. Cries, blood, hellish noises, and stink, she was caught in a loop in time. Always reliving the same visions over again. She deserved it. She had failed. Rocking herself back and forth, on the slick metallic floor she felt Jerome rubbing her head. Yet, she couldn't move her arms, hugging herself as tightly as possible.

"Frankie?" A deep, and masterful voice said, "Frankie!"

She never heard the ring from the little sound the doorbell made. Caught in her mind, a prisoner of her own thoughts that she had not processed yet, she never heard anyone coming in her quarters. She thought it was King for a moment as her eyes were still covered with tears, and had blurred her vision. The moment she wiped them, she realized it was Captain Caldwell. Frankie quickly got on her feet, Jerome still holding on to her head, she said, "Captain." She wasn't too military, despite her recent upgrade in the ship. Frankie tended to be a little looser with the officiality of the title, and ranking, refusing to entirely give in to her new life. It might have made her a bit of a rebel, but she already had a look. She only had to keep her attitude that seemed somewhat okay with her Captain.

Caldwell moved his hands down, to have her sit, "Don't...this is not an official visit." He said with a kind spark in his azure eyes, or at least, as kind as could be from his stern look, "I came here as a friend."

A friend? Frankie never saw him as a friend. A steamy hot commanding human-Walrian hybrid man maybe, but not a friend. "Why?" Frankie asked as she got onto her bed, now holding Jerome in her hands against her chest. She looked at her Captain, searching for a chair to grab for himself. He saw an ergonomic chair, backless, and on wheels. He pulled it toward him, and moved in front of Frankie as he sat down. He leaned forward, trying his best to show his compassion, and asked, "What did you mean by, he looked human?"

Frankie knew it, Caldwell wouldn't be in her room without reason. For the past few days, her memories had been surfacing quite efficiently, and she knew him again. Everyone on board the *Slicer* knew about the ever working, robotic, heartless Captain Caldwell. She rolled her eyes, her head tilting back a little with a fake smile.

"Don't ever present yourself as a friend to me, Caldwell. We both know you named me Commander because you lost your best two in previous missions."

The military was running small onboard Caldwell's ship. Frankie knew, and remembered it clearly. She had doubted her abilities, and usefulness aboard *Slicer* until recently. Then, all memories coming back to her, showing her how much they depended on her, and her skills to accomplish whatever mission it was to recover all Greys' knowledge that somehow got in the hands of the Rakes.

"Everyone knows me as the heartless Captain Caldwell of the LSS *Slicer*." Caldwell said with a grin, "You think I give a fuck about what my crew thinks of me?"

His voice was so cold, that she could've sworn shivers grabbed onto her spine. She heard his tone, strict, and wanting to be heard. She closed her mouth, and listened.

"Everyone might be saying a lot of different things about me. They all know that despite my lack of social skills, I get the job done. For over four years we've been out here trying to bring balance back to this mess of a quadrant without anyone else's help," he said as his index finger pointed toward her door, and then back at her, "They might hate me, or talk behind my back. I don't give a fuck. Why? Because I know they respect me for keeping their own worlds, and timelines safe. In four years, I have lost a total of sixty-three men. Compared to others who lost their people in half a day, and befriended their crew. Who'd you choose in a time of crisis? The one with the smile or the one who has the biggest weapon sitting on one of the beds in his own ship?"

She gulped, needing to swallow her words back, and closed her eyes as she lowered her head. Jerome was now asleep on her lap. She glanced at the Captain, who was watching her new pet sleep.

"I'd choose you over anyone else in the galaxy."

His eyes quickly looked up, and met her own. He shouldn't. She knew it. He hesitated for what seemed like an eternity before she felt the tips of his fingers on both sides of her knees. It had been almost a year now. She knew because it was all coming back to her. Some memories were still suppressed, but they were sometimes surfacing in dreams, sometimes in moments of weaknesses.

"I wouldn't serve or obey anyoneelse's orders."

She felt his touch, shy, and still hesitant. It was as if he didn't know if she was under his command or not. The computer referred to her as a Commander, but her actions spoke otherwise, and had him confused or unaware of what should come next.

"You are a good Captain, Jason Namito Caldwell."

She saw him swallow hard. Looking into the hazel green of her eyes, moving away from the chair, he kneeled before her. His right hand moved away from the side of her knee, close to her face almost as if to try and touch her cheek. She wanted to press his hand to herself, and kiss his palm, but something was preventing them from doing so. Duty? The mission? The fact that they knew each other in a more military manner, yet, felt a strong attraction to one another?

"I've waited for so long to hear those words from you." His voice, commanding, and low, and his head raising as he looked up the wrinkles on his forehead deepening showing his more mature age. "I wanted you to feel comfortable with me. Because I knew you would feel as if you were precious to me, solely for the gift you were given." He looked down, his almond eyes showing his long lashes before he met her gaze again, "At first, I only wanted to protect you, and have you translated their language...then, as I watched you through the main monitor sharing the cameras of the Rakes' ships...I feared for you. I wanted to protect you, and keep you safe."

Frankie wanted to remind him that there was nothing to fear, as she was more than capable of defending herself, but he stopped her. "I saw your mind, and body at work." His eyes widened, and his brows lifted. "I admire you, and your strength. Nobody on this ship took their departure with their world like you did."

Frankie laughed, it was minimal, but a laugh nonetheless. It came through before she used the back of her hand to cover her mouth as she looked outside the window in the infinite darkness of space. She reminded him of the anxiety attacks, PTSD, her OCD, and her germaphobia that constantly immobilized her when facing the truth. Even her IBS was destabilizing, and Dr. Gillman had to feed her through injections to make sure she would get the nutrients she needed.

"You never complained about being away. You did not believe your environment, but you never walked away or rebelled against our mission once you were proven to be in reality." He said, "I also have post-traumatic stress disorder. I deal with it using these as well." He lowered his head, and she followed his hand to his side pocket, and looked at the black container. He opened it. It contained six syringe injections against strong moments of anxiety.

"You are not alone."

Frankie never thought of Captain Caldwell that way. She also knew from watching the crew, and going through episodes herself that he shouldn't be in command of a ship if he was suffering from anxiety or any mental instability. It had her wonder how it was even possible for him to command, and what caused his distress. "Dr. Gillman has known me for the past twenty years. She knows me by heart. She knows that I can function as long as I keep those with me. Of course, if the Alliance would come to know about it, I would be decommissioned, and maybe even court martialed for hiding my mental condition."

Why was he telling her all of this? Frankie couldn't understand why he chose her to bear such a massive secret. There had to be a reason. One thing she knew for sure was that Captain Caldwell never did anything without a motive. All was planned, like a game of chess, he knew the opponent's move before they would, and had it all figured out.

"You know what it is I was told," Frankie said, looking down at him with her head straight, only her eyes staring down. A small grin grew in the corner of his mouth, wrinkles on the side carving into his cheek. "Now you desire nothing more but to know about my past."

His bright azure eyes, almost alien to her, had Frankie re-evaluate her feelings for him. She had wanted to give in to him moments ago. She couldn't lie to herself, she often had indecent thoughts about him. After all, his broad shoulders, strong male appearance, short black hair with some greys on both sides, but his voice, and his hands, had her entirely weak. Everything about him was a vision of a dream to her.

"I don't know what I can do to prove to you that I care about Frank N. Stein. I want to know more about you, and nothing else. Not about your past, or what you saw on that ship unless it brings you peace of mind." Caldwell said in a last attempt to have Frankie open up to him, "Tell me what I must do."

"I'm sorry."

Slowly, Caldwell moved his hands from the side of her knees that now had the coldness of the room. Caressing the fabric, he used the mattress to pull himself up. She missed his touch. Looking up, into the bright blue in his eyes, she praised his strong, and robust posture as he looked down. They both stared at each other for a moment. He gave her his hand, and Frankie took it without any hesitation after moving Jerome onto his little resting nest by the bedside table. She stood up, and followed him around the bed, standing a little closer to her door. His hands moved up to her shoulders, but not quite in contact with her skin that shivered at the simple thought of his fingers caressing her arms. She looked up into his eyes, not wanting to miss one moment of his presence that close to her. She could almost see the most indecent dream she had ever had of the both of them alone together.

*Be careful Frankie, fire is hot, it burns, and it spreads...but like a moth to a flame, of course, I'm heading toward the brightest fire.*

Without ever touching her skin, he moved his hands up, and down her arms, his head leaning forward. She could see his brows meeting as he frowned, and said, "You know, you could have me do anything for you," he said with his low voice, "You could have me start a war in your name." Looking up, his eyes locked on her own, she felt her cheeks warming at the simple thought of his words, and her full lips softly parted, "There's nothing I wouldn't do, just ask me, and I'll give it all to you."

It couldn't be right, she had to wake up. No Captain of a starship would say those words to a...a, abductee...was it Stockholm syndrome? No, because she had been told that she could go home, it just might not be the one she left, and also that the ones they were fighting against might be waiting for her.

"I want," she whispered, before moving a little closer to him. His head leaned forward. He almost touched her forehead. He was now closer to her side near her ear. Frankie on the tip of her toes just to be closer to hear him whisper "Just say it."

At that moment the door opened. No warning. Frankie gasped, and straightened up as Caldwell did the same.

"Frankie?"

# A LIAR IS KING

Commander King stood before Frankie, perplexed his arms on both sides of his body, a frown on his face as he stared at her. She couldn't talk. She didn't know what to say, and wanted Caldwell to explain the situation. She did hope someone would say something, but the tension in the room was so thick, it could've been cut with a knife.

"Thank you, Commander Stein, I will look forward to your report in the morning concerning your encounter with this different looking Rake." He grinned, a spark in his frosty eyes, and walked toward the door, never losing sight of Frankie who subtly shook her head, and smiled in return. '*Unbelievable. Nicely played,*' she thought.

"Commander," Caldwell said with a strong voice.

"Captain," King answered with tight lips, and a grimace.

When the Captain left, and the doors closed, King moved toward Frankie. He lost his anger, yet she could read his worry. He had never liked Caldwell. Yes, he was the first that warned her about the strange behavior of the Captain, but she never thought he would become worried about her being alone with him.

"I do not trust him!" He said while walking around her quarters, "He is...strange, hiding something, and don't get me started on his interest in you."

Of course, Frankie kept her attraction to the Captain to herself. She did not want to reveal how much he appealed to her. She just never knew that it was reciprocated until that night. She moved her black hair behind her ears, hugging herself, and looking down while King kept going on about Captain Caldwell, and his unhealthy obsession with her Grey gene.

"Yet, you let him in your head?" King added as he walked to her, "Don't let him come near you, Frankie. We...I..." He looked down, and Frankie looked up. His thick dark hair now loose went straight down his back, and reflected a blue highlight. His skin had been softly embraced by the sun, and it had her wishing she knew more about him. "I...I want to tell you...shit, it's so hard for me to say."

He wore his fitted Alliance blue-grey shirt, his head leaning forward, and both his hands in his pockets. Frankie tried to make him more comfortable by reaching out to his arm, but instead, King stepped away.

"You know how we've grown close to one another, Frankie."

Yes, King was one of the first onboard *Slicer* to approach Frankie, and helped her feel at home. He was the one who had convinced the second in command to give her quarters of her own because she was the youngest in terms of centuries to be onboard. Yet, Frankie had greater knowledge about specific outer space facts than many who were already aboard the ship. Frankie cherished King's friendship, and nothing more. She had admitted to herself a long time ago finding Captain Caldwell quite attractive. There was no other man in her head ever since she had come on *Slicer*. She thought about Caldwell's feline eyes, his thin lips, and strong jaw. His arms robust, and perfectly cut, just like his pectorals fully developed, and ripped. Then, when looking at King, she noticed something different about him. "It's not like my feelings for Caldwell are new." She saw his lips tightening. King never showed himself to be jealous, worried maybe, but not jealous.

Frankie thought about the many times King had stood up for her when she was still fragile from the abduction. He had defended her when others were mocking not only her species, but her ignorance, and DNA. She had thought maybe Native Americans were not popular among the stars, when in fact, they were envied. She had learned from King when he admitted there were mentions of their respect for extraterrestrials beings among Walrians, and other aliens.

"Nakamo, what is going on, this isn't like you."

He finally lifted his head, looked into her eyes, and replied with a small smile, "Do not have your heart broken by a motherfucking shithead like Captain Caldwell. He is a lie."

His voice deepened, and his feline gaze now seemed more bestial. His posture entirely changed in the time it took for Frankie to blink. She looked at him. But the moment he started walking toward her, she stepped away. Frankie reached for the baseball bat she had the 3D

Photostat make for her, not long after moving onto *Slicer*. Frankie held it tightly in her hands, remembering what her grandfather had taught her. Her eyes on King's temple, she was ready to hit. "Nakamo, what's going on, this is not you. What's wrong with you!" He jumped on her, and she fell down to the ground. His body lay on top of her. He took both her wrists, and spread her arms apart. She quickly moved her legs to hook around his neck, and started squeezing on his jugular. She only needed a few more seconds for him to lose consciousness.

Frankie saw a faint dot in the middle of his pupils...a gold spark. Nobody has a gold dot in the middle of their pupils.

"He...is...a..."

The doors of her quarters opened, and Frankie heard, "Code Hera." She could barely see, still trying to strangle King. She heard two pairs of footsteps running to her, and his voice, filled with worries, "It's okay now, Commander," he said after calling for security.

She finally released the tension in her legs, looking into Caldwell's eyes with tears taking over. He winked, and turned his attention to the four guards who had quickly responded to the Captain's calling. "Take Commander King to the medical facility. I will follow soon." Holding King in manacles, both his hands placed in front of him with a metal bar going up his neck, and attaching to a collar surrounding it, they answered, "Aye, Captain!"

Frankie heard him, "He is a lie!" King followed it quickly with, "Don't let him fool you!" His voice slowly became an echo, and then he was gone. Dr. Gillman, still present, was about to take a look at Frankie, Caldwell said, "Would you please give us a moment alone, Doctor?" Dr. Gillman left Frankie's quarters, and the doors closed. She looked into Caldwell's eyes, kneeling by her side, both his hands on his knees. His eyes, merely staring at her with affection, and she could see they were covered by a soft veil of water. Still lying on the ground, Frankie quickly lifted herself up, and wrapped her arms around him.

Frankie had her fingers digging into his shoulder blades while her head rested on his chest before she pulled herself up a little more. Frankie pressed her cheek against his ear, and held him tight, as if never wanting him to let go. Finally, she felt his arms closing in on her. He murmured, "It's okay. I'm here now. No one will ever hurt you. I promise."

Tears rolling down her face, Frankie thought about the horrible images that only played in her mind like a movie. Never had she ever thought King would attack her, and try to...no, that was not the King

Frankie knew. She refused to believe it. He would have never done that to her.

"How did you know?" She moved her head away from Caldwell and frowned. She had not pushed the panic button or called for help. Frankie wondered if Caldwell noticed something was different with the Commander when leaving her quarters. "Answer me. How did you know?" She was about to let go of Caldwell, but he held on to her tighter, "The more you doubt me, the more you develop paranoia!" He held her in place, and asked Frankie to let him explain what happened.

"When I left, I was about to go to my quarters to take a shower and go to bed." Frankie closed her eyes, this was not the time to imagine the Captain naked. She had thousands of emotions rolling through her head. "I was stopped by Wolf who told me that Cadet Zwally had detected a strange pattern in the Decoder's history that required my attention."

Frankie knew that they usually would have gone to Alaska, but "Leclerc was already on the spot. Cadet Zwally realized, when doing her shift's report, and diagnosis that the Decoder recorded a sequence that wasn't from anyone's DNA record onboard *Slicer*. It was attached to King's genetic code." Caldwell let go of Frankie, who surprised herself by holding onto one of Caldwell's hands, and he continued explaining, "At first, Wolf contacted Dr. Gillman, and thought it might have been a virus. Leclerc was still performing advanced diagnostics, and Dr. Gillman was running analysis. When all was said and done, they both had come to a frightening conclusion." Frankie feared for the worst when tightening her grip on Caldwell, he completed, "Commander King carries the Rake mutation."

Frankie shook her head, "No." She refused to believe it. She was the one who had left him on the bridge, following her instinct to go to the dark room. Frankie knew that if she would've stayed with him, they could've fought their way out. Caldwell stopped her, and took her hands away from her face. "Look at me! Frankie, look at me!" Lowering himself, his eyes looking up into her own, she noticed the lines on his forehead carving in, and then, she followed the line of his straight nose down to his fine lips, "For all we know, what you did saved his life." It was easier to blame herself, but he said, "Frankie. You would've been surrounded by at least twenty Rakes in a hurry to feed on your blood and flesh. There was no way, not even you, could have killed them all. By striking a deal with that one Rake, you saved King from being eaten alive, and the same fate awaited you."

She had a hard time looking at him. Her vision was entirely blurred by the pain she felt. Thousands of scenarios, all worse than the next took place in her head as to what King could become. She thought about the past, her missions with King, and her friendship with Wolf, Alaska, and Dr. Gillman. She remembered the death of other officers, and almost losing King at the hands of the Rakes. She remembered the picture, and now...King trying to either abuse her or eat her because he carried the Rake mutation in him.

Frankie looked around her, and felt her meerkat coming near her. Her pet must have been sleeping through the entire episode. She knew that despite being a meerkat, Jerome was the laziest one she had ever seen. Not that alert, and more like an actual cat. She felt his head near her hair, and said, "Nakamo said you were a lie." She stared into the frost of Caldwell's eyes, "You said you would do anything for me, was that a lie?"

"No."

She had her head leaning against the mattress, her body entirely stripped of any residual strength. With a broken voice, she asked Caldwell, "Then give me what I want, the truth...why did he say you were a lie?"

"Because I am."

A smile in the corner of his mouth, his hand still held by Frankie as she nodded, "Good because I am too."

# THE ENCOUNTER

The next day, Frankie was in the medical facility by King's side. He was in a stasis chamber. The plastic-like cylinder measured about 2.7 meters tall and had a diameter of a little over a meter. The thick liquid inside must have been transparent but reflected the blue light from the inside. King was in his dark fitted underwear. His body floated in the artificial amniotic liquid that allowed him to breathe without a mask.

She looked at him, the glass allowing her to see her friend from head to toe. Only a few wires were attached to him, and needles were stabilized in his veins. Probably artificially fed, King resembled a fetus in a womb.

"Why don't you go back to your quarters, Frankie? I'll let you know when I know more." Dr. Gillman's skin had some hexagon designs varying in flesh colors, a little like a Savannah monitor lizard. Some being lighter than others, under the black light of the medical facility at the time, they were illuminated like little stars.

"What is happening to him, Doctor?" In front of one of the monitors on the side of the stasis chamber, Dr. Gillman showed her the DNA structure of King. "The Rake's somatic mutation sequence is slowly reforming King's many short stretches of nucleotides, and I can't seem to be able to find a way to stop it." Frankie looked at Dr. Gillman's face now leaning forward, her long fingers and claws slowly slid down the monitor. "I fear that now it will attack specific genes such as protein, and others that are primordial to an organism. It is rewriting his DNA structure rapidly."

Frankie's eyes were now blurry, and she knew they might have been almost lime green as they changed with her emotions. The more she cried, the greener they became. She heard the door of the medical bay opening, and Dr. Gillman excused herself. Frankie turned to the glass, and saw the slow change in King's skin, yet no pattern seemed to stick. Then, all turned black for a moment when she touched
the glass.

*What's happening... what happened to Slicer?*

The room was dark. Everything surrounding Frankie was floating as if there was no gravity. The only lights were from the secondary system used when a ship was to be abandoned. Her feet were still on the ground, and she wondered how she was not floating like the equipment that wasn't attached around her in a zero-gravity environment.

Technically, she shouldn't have been able to breathe. Frankie was quite aware of being in a dream until she realized it was too real. This wasn't a dream but something else. A communication of some kind, maybe like a telepathic link? She walked around to the central medical station in the middle of the room. The white circular multiple monitor screen displayed all different variations of vital systems from every alien onboard. It could also be used to access crewmembers' medical, and psychological files, and show recent medical or again, psychological analysis or tests.

Frankie touched the screen with her index finger. It was still working, meaning she could access specific files. Over the past year, she had been able to familiarize herself with the Alliance technology and learn their "Galaxian" chosen language. She entered her name, nothing. She then typed the first name that came to mind.

"Captain Jason Namito Caldwell. Human from Earth. Badge of Honor for display of courage in the Battle of Giza. Held Top Secret: Mention of Bravery in Division 8 Unit Recovery First Abduction of

2504. Ready to sacrifice his life not to reveal Galaxy Safety Undisclosed Information...but I want his physical, and mental status," Frankie thought.

Frankie scrolled down, and finally saw what she wanted.

"Ah! Caldwell. Born August 31st, 2472. Currently 42 years old. Genetically enhanced with Walrian genes. 1.9 meters. A hundred, and five kilos. Black hair. Blue eyes...okay, what about...what?" She read more carefully, "Born of a Cree mother, and Irish father. Last descendant of the Caldwell family founders of CaldTech Industries."

Some other information showed Caldwell with scars on his back. It mentioned being from the first battle when he was captured from years before they met. She read his psychological file, and read aloud, "Suffers from night terrors, and insomnia leading to paranoia. Shows definitive signs of PTSD. Captain Jason Namito Caldwell is not fit for duty."

The data showed 2504. Frankie knew, from other crew members including King, that Caldwell never stopped his function as a Captain. In fact, his records didn't show any other ranks. Some years were missing from when he was a Commander, Lieutenant, Cadet, something!

A noise was heard coming from the corridor. Frankie decided to grab an empty syringe usually kept under the monitors and attached it to a tranquilizer tube. She had enough to take down a T Rex. Frankie strolled to the door, following the monitor station before crawling alongside the wall to the entrance. She looked up.

"Fuck," she whispered, then blocked her mouth with her empty hand. She couldn't stop staring, yet she wished she would close her eyes. What was happening? Where was she? Was she receiving telepathic communication with another being because this seemed like a directed, yet tangible memory. Everything surrounding her was real. The touch, texture, nothing was blurred or out of her control. Clear as day, Frankie could recognize her surroundings. The only difference being that it seemed from a different time. She guessed, before her arrival on board *Slicer*.

The crew member, one she had never seen before, was pinned to the ceiling, with large nails from a gun she assumed by the strong impalement of it. The body, inert, was not decomposed but frozen by the lack of life support. His eyes were out of their sockets, while the mouth was deprived of a tongue, and nor were there ears on each side of his face.

"Rakes."

She was about to follow the corridor, but first took a deep breath, and then stopped. "Wait...these colors aren't right. *Slicer* crew members wore charcoal, and silver, not black, and gold."

Then a voice was heard in a light whisper, "Nothing begins. Nothing ends."

The black light was still on, King in the stasis chambers. Frankie looked around, and slowly touched her forehead to see if she had a fever. She saw Dr. Gillman walking toward her accompanied by the Captain. In his uniform, still on duty, she saw a shy smile, and a wink. Somehow, it was comforting to her that he seemed to be the same man he was the night before in her quarters. She remembered him holding her hand until she had fallen asleep. A very light sleeper, she felt him pick her from the ground, and put her in bed beneath her sheets. She remembered because ever since one specific event from her past, she had never slept the same. She even could've sworn he gave her a kiss on her forehead before leaving.

"Commander Stein." He said, she bowed, and replied with a cold voice,

"Captain." About to leave, she heard the Doctor mentioned her being immobile her eyes fixing nothing for a moment. Gillman added that no stimuli could snap her out of the daydream she seemed captured within. Gillman added that she worried about those black bags under her eyes, Frankie took the opportunity, "I just need some sleep. I haven't entirely recovered from the encounter with the Rakes. That's all. Nothing to worry about."

She left the medical facility and headed toward engineering where she knew Alaska would be ending her shift. She stalked toward the elevator but found herself stuck inside with one female she wished she had never met, Admiral Aino Heikki. She was one who had experienced some steamy adventures with Caldwell.

"So, still trying to have Jason all to yourself?"

The female Nordic could be mistaken easily for any regular human, had it not been for her bigger eyes, and slightly more full head. She had natural white blonde hair, straight, and slick, but tied in a ponytail. Her eyes were grey, and her skin was the fairest Frankie had ever seen.

"You know he is mine," she said. Annoyed, Frankie would have broken her throat just to stop hearing her voice. "I'm warning you," The female alien added.

Arriving at the engineering floor level, the door opened. Frankie decided to turn, and look at the female alien puzzled, "Excuse me, what's your name again?" The Nordic alien frowned, and ground her teeth while Frankie smiled, and left the elevator. She walked toward engineering, about to enter the 'rotary meat plow.' The whole floor, like the rest of the ship, was in the colors of dark grey, white, and black. The engineering deck had a metallic grid as a floor in case of fluid accumulation from the biomechanical bags inside the walls. On each side against the wall, were meter-long metal plates before it went back to its nanofiber construction. The corridor itself had a rotating blade system, reminiscent of snow plow, meant to stabilize the magnetic field from engineering and the rest of the ship. The corridor itself was in fact a separator between the engine and the front of the ship, for numerous safety protections.

People were moving around, trying to repair the FTL (faster than light engine.) She heard Alaska ordering her team around, "I want a full diagnostic on the hyperspace backup system. I don't care when you finish it, just call me when you're done. We need out of here!"

Alaska had ended her shift five minutes ago, leaving her second in command to run the night shift. Everyone was on edge, since they were still in Rake Space. The ship held in place, as much as it could. But they were drifting without the FTL engine permitting them to leave danger in a blink of an eye, but so far, no luck. *Slicer* was a sitting duck, hence, why Alaska wanted at least the STL or slower than light system back online.

The stabilizer still holding, Alaska ordered her night shift team to work on the maintenance of all primordial systems. She asked for the cleaning team, doing their job in the mechanical section to keep up the good work. Their work was also impeccable in the engine rooms, preventing *Slicer* from suffering more damage caused by blockages or the lack of lubricant.

"Frankie?" She heard her best friend say, but she seemed to disappear. "Frankie are you, all right?" Her voice was only an echo.

*Slicer* was once again in some sort of safety mode. The lights were off, only the security lighting was on, sometimes flashing, and unstable. The neon lights were dispersed and had 2.5 meters in between each setting. The room was not much different than what she was used to. Monitor screens on both sides of the walls in the main engineering room were built-in, and the keyboards for some would come out at the touch of the screen. The open room above had the secondary server farm, protected by a tall and wide anti-bombing wall. It was solely for engineering, and secondary aspects of the ship, but were still very important.

Frankie knew the engine room was about ten decks down, controlled from a safe place. Only the cleaning crew, and certified engineers, such as Alaska had the right to access the engine deck itself. Frankie had never seen it from the inside, and neither had the Captain, as it was solely for those with the required knowledge.

At the moment, all of the monitor screens had cracks, and the floor was almost completely covered in soot, almost as if an explosion had occurred. She could hear screams from afar. They sounded as if they were all around, and yet, no one was there. The ship was empty. The odor of burned plastic, and wires were carried by a breeze she didn't know the provenance of, and almost scorched the inside of Frankie's nostrils. She walked toward the back of the ship but heard a loud cry behind her. The voice was male, growly, and almost out of breath. She walked towards the sound she heard, thinking it was coming from one of the big Decoder rooms.

Frankie thought she recognized the voice. She started running, holding onto the syringe, ready to use it if someone would appear before her. *Wait, I still have a syringe, how is that possible? Is this a memory?* The corridor was curving, and on the other side would be the Decoder room. She placed her thumb before the scanner, but it didn't recognize her prints. *So, this is a memory, but it is dating back to before I came aboard.*

"I'm from another time. I'm either walking in a memory from the ship, or I see what will come to pass. The syringe is a symbol, it must mean something." Frankie thought aloud as she felt it to be too real to be a dream, and certainly had to be a continuation of earlier, it couldn't be a coincidence. She was able to read. Her vision was not blurred, and she had strength. These things usually did not remain so in her dreams. Now that her Grey gene was at full capacity, she logically thought that whatever was trying to communicate with her felt it important to pass on this memory or data to her.

"What if the ship is part organic? Alaska often said that compared to other *Slicer* blueprints, *Slicer* was different, and had an entirely singular interface. She even reported that it would shift commands on its own before an overload would occur." Frankie even remembered Alaska asking the Captain for the right to dismantle the engine, but he never granted her the right to do so. "Is *Slicer* a decoy?" Frankie almost forgot why she stood before the door of the Decoder room, until she heard another loud scream. Again, sounding like an echo, the voice seemed almost distant, and ghostly. It almost had her swear she was walking through a memory of the ship.

How could she get in? The ship might have gone through a battle. It did look abandoned, but the RS, also known as the Recognizing System, was still functional. She couldn't bust through the doors as they were reinforced titanium. She looked around and remembered the body that was stapled to the ceiling a few meters back. Frankie decided to run toward the torn body, his flesh, frozen in the emptiness of space of a drifting battle cruise ship. Frankie bent over and took out her knife that she kept in her military looking boots alongside her leg. She looked up to the body, noticed his eyes, and tongue gone again, and said, "fucking Rakes." She took a deep breath, and was about to take the hand of the human man attached to the ceiling. She looked at the large, and full steel staples holding him, and realized she had never cut or amputated a human before. "No wonder we're all fucked up, fucking wars."

Frankie had to fight everything within her when reaching for the hand over her head. She pressed the touchscreen monitor and requested a horizontal ladder. Beneath the screen a ladder ejected, and Frankie stepped on it to reach the body above her. She held the thumb with her own, and her index finger. Placing her blade against the flesh of the dead, she pulled back, and swung. The thumb was now in her hand. She fought back her gag reflex, and ran back to the Decoder room.

Frankie placed the thumb before the scanning device, hoping the mutilated man was a Decoder officer, and closed her eyes for a moment. She wanted to forget about what she had just done. She needed to ignore the feeling of her blade cutting through the flesh, tendons, ligaments, veins, and bones of another human being. Dead or not, Frankie never thought she would have had to do that, and she hoped to never have to do it again.

The doors swung open, but there was no light shining through. Frankie felt a sudden urge to run away, but something inside her was convinced answers lay in the darkness of the ship. She heard screams of terror, a rough, and stretched out male voice crying. An echo of what has been. Frankie walked toward the Decoder receiver and stood in front of a place where motion sensor lights should have been. Nothing.

She walked to the back of the room to access the computer, when a single light turned on by itself. Frankie could see it by the reflection on the monitor's screen the size of the entire upper wall equalled to 2.4 meters. One man was suspended in the middle of where the Decoder sequence would have released the dematerialization process capable through the blue light that was on. Frankie didn't understand the entire science behind it. She only knew that those lights had a role to play in the decoding process of the teleportation device.

The reflection of the light, the silhouette of the man. Frankie knew who she would see, and she was afraid of turning around. Very slowly, Frankie moved her eyes as her head turned toward the device. There was Caldwell's body being stretched by the Decoder. Someone had been tampering with the teleportation machine. She was told by Wolf once that the Decoder could have been used as a weapon, if one would only rematerialize one part, and not the other. It felt like losing a limb. The pain was very intense, and would be almost unbearable. Frankie wondered who could cause all this pain.

There was no one else aboard the ship. Had Caldwell been caught in a sequence until *Slicer* was rescued? Frankie approached the Captain, and saw his arm materializing. She touched it, and for a moment, his fingers held on to her. Was it somewhere written that she would relive the memory, or was it another symbolic gesture or moment?

"It can't be. I can speak, I can think. I am feeling texture, and I feel my own weight. This isn't just an illusion. I'm walking through someone else's memory."

"No. You're walking through something's memory."

Hair standing straight up on her neck, Frankie quickly turned, and held the syringe ready to plant it into anyone prepared to attack.

"King?" She screamed so loud her voice cracked, and she shouted, "Tutankhaten!"

Her body was substantial, and her eyes could barely see. Her head was leaning back, and she felt as if she had been stabbed on her left side. Frankie tried to speak, but her throat felt dry, and irritated. "A... Ala...ska."

She felt her body being moved against a muscular torso. Arms wrapped around her, in between her legs. She lifted her head, and could see Captain Caldwell's neck, and jaw from below. She saw him looking to the side, ordering Dr. Gillman to hurry. He asked everybody to stay away and make room. Only Alaska was allowed to come with them.

He looked down at her, and said, "All is okay, Commander. I came as soon as I heard."

Everything faded to black. Nothing made sense in her mind after her eyes closed and she fell into a deep sleep. Frankie woke up in her own bed. Surprised to not have been in the medical facility, she looked to her side, and saw her meerkat, Jerome, curled up next to her. "I was going to see Alaska to tell her what happened. What I saw, and what I felt. I wanted her to know about Ash, and about the visions I've been having." Tears building up in her eyes, she cursed the gene she had been given before rolling on her side to pet her meerkat. "I'm lost, Jerome. I don't know what to do."

She felt as if someone was in her room. She felt a strong presence and quickly straightened up. She grabbed the baseball bat at the end of her bed which had been there since King's sudden psychosis episode. She held it in her hands, just like her grandfather had taught her, and straightened up on her bed.

Frankie slowly moved, one leg down, then the other. It was dark in her quarters, and when she approached the armchair, she saw Caldwell. His head was leaning to one side, and his body was entirely relaxed. He was sitting forward, as if trying to be comfortable, both his arms resting on the edge of the chair. He was asleep. His eyes closed, she watched him slowly breathing. His chest moving slowly as he took a breath, and gently let it out.

His lips were somewhat parted, and she heard a small, subtle snore. Frankie relaxed her arms and smiled. It was the kind of smile a woman gives when looking at a man she had been dreaming of for so long, finally getting closer to him in a very romantic way. She assumed he was off duty, as Caldwell wore his loose black jogging pants, and a dark grey tank top. It showed his muscular arms, and large, strong hands.

Something dropped from his right hand as his fingers slowly relaxed, and let go. A white gold chain with a cross fell to the ground. Frankie put the baseball bat down against the other armchair and crouched next to Caldwell without a sound. She picked up the chain she recognized as her own, and lifted her eyes up to stare at him, sleeping.

Another small snore, she chuckled silently, and sat down, her body against the side of her other chair. She reached out to his hand, entirely loose, and relaxed, and touched his fingers. She remembered how safe she felt when he held her hand the night King changed for someone she didn't know. He had comforted her. He had made sure she was safe. She placed her hand in his, and felt his fingers closing on her. She looked at his eyes, but they never opened. He still snored, and she felt her body becoming heavy, her eyes burned as she felt the desire to sleep. She moved closer to Caldwell, his legs spread apart. She placed her head on his lap, facing outward, and looked at her hand in his, and slowly closed her eyes.

A tear rolled down her face. Frankie was afraid to see another vision of Caldwell being tortured. *Slicer* had some residual hauntings, and she could feel it. Frankie blamed it on her Grey gene that had changed her life for the worse. Frankie suddenly felt fingers running through her hair, slowly, and gently. She moved his hand closer to her face, and kissed his fingers, one by one. Frankie kept his hand close to her face, as to have him keep her, and with his thumb he caressed her cheek. His fingers gently played with her hair. She closed her eyes and moved her legs. With her knees up to her chin, she made sure his other hand would keep close to her chest.

"You can't tell me you are comfortable." He said, in a quiet voice. Graver than usual, but she didn't want to move, "Why don't you move up here?" He moved to bring her onto his lap, but Frankie feared it might take away the perfect moment they shared.

"It is very confusing to know you want me just as much as I want you, and yet, every time I show more affection, you pull back." She listened to him, caressing his hand, his fingers still playing with her hair. "It was instant with us, Frankie. We looked at each other, and we knew somehow, you and I would happen. I know you did, because I felt it too." It might have been tough for him to say, it would be for any man, but she could tell by his voice he was still sleepy. "You know me. It's been over four years. When will it happen?"

Caldwell knew how attracted she was to him, for all the time she had felt her cheeks warming in his presence, and the deep breaths she would take when he would walk too close to her. Frankie also knew he was longing to hold her and kiss her. It was evident by the way Caldwell would look at her, the grin in the corner of his mouth when walking away, turning his head to make sure she still looked at him. He would sometimes make sure they would bump into each other, and made many excuses to visit her quarters.

"It started by me listening to you, talking about your life as a writer for a reputable blog in your spare time. You said you worked for Cald-Tech Industries as a computer programmer. That you were not special in any way." She heard him chuckle, his fingers still moving a strand of her hair from one finger to the other, "It took you some time to let me approach you. You wouldn't see the psychiatrist we have on board, as recommended by Dr. Gillman, because he reminded you of a spider, and you have arachnophobia. You refused every help we had, but me."

Frankie recalled the moment she had let Caldwell in her life. The moment she allowed him to pass her doorstep, and walk in. Commander King was still someone she wasn't ready to talk to at the time. Frankie remembered the anxiety, the never-ending feeling of being in a constant state of fear. Cardiophobia stepping in, she needed the relaxant, and the many other drugs that Caldwell would bring, along with Dr. Gillman. Pills not being popular in the twenty-sixth century, injections were thought to be more effective, and less addictive.

"Do you remember the very first night we met?" He whispered as they sat in the darkness.

1700 Hours, 24th of October 2506
(Gregorian calendar,)

# A.D WAYNE

Milky Way Galaxy, Orion Constellation, Earth.
North America, Canada, Quebec, Aurora.

At twenty-six, Frankie mostly worked from home as a blogger, and aspiring author. Formerly a computer programmer, she had worked for one of the most technologically advanced companies. When a fire broke out in her department, and she was exiting the building, she had fallen down the stairs. She ended up breaking her right leg, and injuring her lower back, and right wrist.

Not used being on a sabbatical, Frankie had quickly found a way to occupy herself, and that was writing about a subject she knew quite a bit about. One summer night, after eating sushi in her secluded cottage house up in Aurora, she saw some unexplainable lights coming from outside. In her living room, Frankie turned off the documentary about alien visitors. Moving her blanket away, as her house was cool from the AC, she heard some rather strange thunder. Turning on her vegan leather couch, she looked out the window, and stared at the materializing bodies.

"What the fuck?"

It was a quiet street; there were a lot of trees, and a few neighbors were located sparsely in between. The town was known for its many unexplainable stories, but Frankie had never lived one of her own. Her house had a long driveway, many mature trees in the front yard blocked her view. She placed her glasses right and watched the materialization of what seemed to be beings.

"I guess the answer is Alien?" She wondered.

There was some sort of rumbling coming from above, but nothing natural. A trio of humanoid people appeared. She couldn't take her eyes off them. One tall male, and two shorter females. Frankie tried to stay low, but she knew whatever those aliens wanted, no matter how hard she would try to hide, they would get to her if that was their mission. She watched them walk up her driveway, and her heart started beating faster. Quickly Frankie grabbed onto her bottle of anxiety pills and popped one out. Cardiophobia was one of her many mental problems. Feeling her heart racing caused her more pain than fear. The doorbell rang. There were only two logical options. One, answer the door and let the aliens in or two, do not answer the door and let them take it down. Either way, the aliens won. Frankie managed to pull herself up and walked to her front door to open it with a big fake smile.

One female had silky midnight brown skin, long black braided hair going down her right shoulder, and a long slender neck. She wore a light red summer dress with sandals. She was tall, and quite slim, but Frankie could tell by her sharp shoulders, and biceps that she was athletic. There was a shorter woman, no taller than five feet and a couple of inches, graduated bob haircut black as the night, and very pale skin. She had a curvy body and wore a dark purple tank top with white loose lounge pants. Her icy green eyes inspired trust, and Frankie feared she just might trust the alien. When looking up behind the brunette, she saw a tall man with skin the color of gold. A sly look to his eyes, she was hypnotized by the darkness of his irises, but then took a glance at his thick black hair, braided, and coming down both sides of his neck. He wore a light grey v-neck tee, and jeans. He looked as if he had walked out of a dream. One thing she knew, he reminded her of family she had in Kahnawake.

"Who are you?" Frankie asked, "What are you doing here?"

She had not invited them inside her house, yet. After all, despite her martial arts knowledge, there was no way she could defend herself against three alien people. The anxiety pill took effect. She got a little dizzy, but at least she could not hear or feel her heart in her chest anymore. She kept herself between the entrance door and the wall waiting for an answer from one of the aliens.

"We are here to talk to you," the short female said with a bright smile. Quickly, the taller female said that there was no use lying, and that's when the man stepped in, "We are here to ask you to come with us to the LSS *Slicer*. We are from the future, well, we're all from different futures, and the tall one here with an inhuman long neck, is an alien posing as a human, because she looks like one. She's also our doctor."

"What kind of barbarian torture device is this on your leg, and arm, my poor sweetheart!" The bronze skin woman asked with a frown and wanting to touch her cast.

Strangely, that's when Frankie let them inside her home. The alien doctor brought her back to a scene of one of her favorite sci-fi movies. They sat on her couch in the living room and asked what had happened to her. She explained the fire at CaldTech Industries, and then used her left side to try, and sit. The tall man presented himself as Commander Nakamo King, and helped her sit down.

"We have the best doctors on board our ship, here as an African American looking lady is the head of the medical facility. This appearance is the closest to human the projectors could achieve using Cadet Zwally as a reference. Her name is Dr. Gillman. She works wonders." His voice was just as dreamy as his looks, and Frankie almost felt embarrassed that he met her in her favorite sci-fi cartoon tank top about a mad grandpa scientist and his grandson, and a puppet eating cookies character on her sports pajama bottoms. Her black curly hair was held up in a very messy bun held by a lime green scrunchy, almost falling off the side of her head, and she wore nerdy glasses. Despite her excellent vision, working at the computer for long hours could give her migraines. The glasses helped with the glare of the computer. "I'm sure you'll like her," he added with a smile grin.

The other woman presented herself as Lieutenant Alaska Leclerc. She explained that she was from the twenty-seventh century, and had an appearance a little different than others due to her being a hybrid. "My mother was not entirely human." She then added, "We are here because we know that you were abducted when you were young and experimented on. Humans have a long history of encounters with the Greys." Then, her memory faded, and Frankie lost consciousness. When she woke up she was somewhere she never thought she would be.

"Do you understand me, Frank Stein?"

Her voice was clear, formal, and serious. She looked humanoid, but her reptilian eyes with sideway lids closing, and opening like one of a crocodile gave her a different look than humans of Earth. She might have had no hair, but her slim neck, with a Savannah, lizard-like patterns added to her unique beauty such as Frankie had never seen before. Her skin was a mix of peach, sand, and a little navy blue. It even had a very subtle, almost unnoticeable, little white dots spread around.

She asked if Frankie understood her for a second time. All she did was look up into her reptilian eyes, and nodded, still debating if she should believe they were the good guys of a friendly 'Planet Federation,' or ones of a cyborg invading empire.

"What am I doing here?" Frankie managed to ask with a trembling voice.

The reptilian female approached Frankie, and helped her step down from the octagon pedestal with three-quarter rings of flashing faint lights. What seemed to be three security guards, in metallic blue uniforms wearing black helmets saluted her as she followed the alien to the corridor.

"I'm Dr. Amani Gillman, and I work for the Liberty Military. This is my true organic form." As Frankie followed her, she observed the hallway that was built in a material she had never seen before, and although it seemed as hard as metal, it was somewhat soft to the touch, "Nanofiber. It's built to be extra solid, and yet, shock absorbent, perfect for interstellar traveling, and unwanted encounters." Dr. Gillman said, noticing her interest.

The lighting was bright, and the environment was completely sterile. Numerous computer screens were constantly displaying the status of the ship, and its different compartments. Frankie looked back to front, still following Dr. Gillman who stopped by a wall that opened to an elevator.

"Why am I here?" Frankie asked, but the doctor repeated the same reason the trio gave her some time ago. "Is this a close encounter of the 4th kind, or are you going to clone me by extracting my DNA? I'm visited by beings that aren't native to Earth, and asked for my help. I mean, what is a girl like me to conclude from that?" Frankie asked, uncomfortable but with a smile. She tried to hide her anxiety, but her pills weren't designed to keep her calm when abducted by aliens. There was a knot forming in her stomach.

Frankie's breathing suddenly shortened. She felt a burning ball of fire pushing its way up to her throat. Her vision was abruptly blurred by tears, and she found herself paralyzed by fear. The truth was, Frankie didn't know what was going to happen to her, and what she was doing on that spaceship. In Frankie's head, in her way of understanding space travel, one had to master traveling through space and time to achieve such a distance between planets. So, she was either literally going crazy, or she was on board a spaceship about to become an abductee. Once she was back on Earth, no one would ever believe her.

Both Frankie's arms hugging herself, leading back against the elevator wall, she pushed little cries of panic, feeling her heart pounding in her chest. "It's anxiety, you're going to be okay," The doctor said patiently. Frankie tried to convince herself too, trying to control her panic attack. Deprived of the medication she carried with her in case of such a physical reaction...heck, she never had a physical response that traumatizing, not many did.

"Miss Stein, you're okay." The doctor repeated, as she saw her pointing what looked like a thick laser at her. There was a slow wide range white flashing light. The doctor looked at the screen monitor by Frankie using it as a medical monitor, she guessed. "You're experiencing an anxiety attack. You seem to suffer from chronic anxiety. I will give you a relaxant. Come with me."

The elevator door opened. Dr. Gillman never answered Frankie's questions. Her breathing shortened again, and Frankie refused to follow her. She pushed Dr. Gillman away, and was about to run when the three security guards from the room showed up and blocked the passageway. Frankie screamed, and fell onto her knees, her hands holding her head as she envisioned the worst possible scenario.

"No one is going to hurt you, Frankie." A small voice said as she held onto her hands, her eyes forcefully closed that she couldn't see the face of the person speaking. "This is a rescue mission." The stranger pulled Frankie toward her chest, and held her in her arms, "You are of Earth in the 21st century. I'm also of Earth, but from the twenty-seventh century, and we are all part of the Space-Time Liberty Defense to keep order in time, and dimensions."

Her hand petting Frankie's head, she kept crying in horror, afraid of what was awaiting her. The female's voice somehow brought Frankie some comfort as she said, "We need you, Frankie. Captain Caldwell needs you to guide us."

Frankie lifted her head up slowly, and looked at her fair skin with light blue hieroglyph markings, then into her bright green eyes, and said, "Alaska?"

Then, a tall silhouette walked against the lighting of the ceiling. He stayed in the dark until he crouched by Alaska and Frankie's side, and said with a soft, but husky voice, "I'm Captain Jason Namito Caldwell. We are here to protect you, Frank N. Stein." She was lost in his frosty blue gaze, and listened to him when he said, "I will never let anything happen to you, I promise."

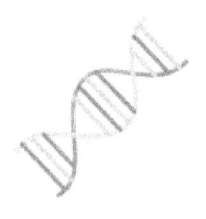

Her head against his lap, his fingers running through her hair, she was about to fall asleep when she heard him say, "I guess I have failed." He felt guilty. That was the reason why he had been at her side for the last few nights, and the last two missions. He felt remorseful, and it was eating him up from the inside. "I promised I would protect you, and yet, those motherfucking mind fuckers got to you, and erased your memories twice." Frankie remembered, they weren't able to take her down, so they used a hand device that targeted her short-term memory.

She lifted her head the moment he stopped playing with her hair and looked at him. Never had she seen Caldwell on the verge of tears. She held his hand, and he moved toward her, near her, so close she could feel his warm breath on her skin. "I wanted to protect you. I wanted to keep you to myself. This ship, this crew, this timeline, and all the others, have to get in line behind me, because I claimed you first."

Frankie stared into the eyes of the Captain. He let himself slide off the armchair and onto his knees. As she looked at the lines on his forehead caving in when he raised his eyebrows, he said, "I was sent to rescue you before the Rakes, or the others would have abducted you. I —" Frankie interrupted Caldwell.

"I see memories of the ship. This starship is haunted by a brutal past. I thought I was crazy at first, but then it kept on happening. I think it is the Grey gene in me that is sensitive to what this ship is capable of doing. Whatever time it has seen, whatever place in this galaxy it has visited, somewhere down the line you were tortured, and it nearly killed you. What am I doing here?"

# THE SUPERIOR LIFE

Caldwell took Frankie to the cargo area, and asked all security personnel to leave them alone. The cargo deck was fifteen floors below the main bridge in the cleaver shaped starship. There were five different cargo areas, and each section had a specific purpose. They were used for stocking goods such as water, oxygen tanks, and medical supplies, which also included nutrient injections in case of emergencies. However, there was that one cargo room that had security guarding the place around the clock. It was the one place that was completely off limits to anyone except the Captain.

When Caldwell, and Frankie walked past the curve, she recognized the passageway, and she stopped with a gasp. The images in her head surfaced like a photo album she had just flipped open. Hands holding her mouth, her eyes rounded. Caldwell looked where her eyes were fixed, and she heard his voice as his hand rubbed her back. "His name was Carl Rosenburg. He was the chief security officer before Commander King took charge." Frankie's eyes slowly moved to her right to see Caldwell pointing exactly where she remembered the man she cut the thumb from. "He fought many Rakes before, um...that happened to him. We were on our ninth day of fighting with those fuckers."

Frankie didn't know if she would have preferred to have gone officially insane or know that she was sharing the ship's memories. She wondered if she would soon start seeing ghosts as well. When Caldwell placed his thumb in front of the scanner, Frankie remembered the dead one she used, but she couldn't say anything. They walked together into the cargo area and saw the Decoder. Those Decoders were used to transfer equipment and provisions to the ship. Unlike relocating organic beings, those Decoders were solely used for materialistic purposes.

Frankie didn't understand, she saw Caldwell being tortured with that exact Decoder. She recognized the walls, the monitors, the Decoder itself, and could relive the precise memory. She was left with shivers going up her spine to the back of her neck.

"I was tortured by one of the Rakes' Generals. His name was Ash Zachariah." He pointed at the Decoder, "He had me placed on a... um... a" Caldwell had a hard time speaking the words out loud. He was scratching his head, and staring at the ground.

Frankie was emotional thinking about what he was going through inside his head.

She moved her hand to hold his. She stepped toward him, as he said without looking at her, as if to have not her see him weak, "Are you familiar with the rack?" Frankie nodded.

0500 Hours, 04th of October 2506
(Gregorian calendar,)
Milky Way Galaxy, Orion Constellation, Pluto *Slicer,* Cargo 05.
Invasion: Day 10.
Ship status: Sustainable.
Loss: 32.

"You have held your tongue for far too long, Caldwell, is it?" He was young, tall, and strong looking. He had a human appearance, but Caldwell knew better. They all looked like humans once. "You want to be human? Well, let's remind you of what they used to be made out of, shall we?"

Caldwell was held on his knees, and the right side of his head bleeding after a hit with the blunt side of an ax. His hands were tied together in a straitjacket manner, so he couldn't even attempt to defend himself. He looked to his left side, at the Rakes moving a 2.1-meter wooden ladder, with the steps being flat instead of horizontal to be climbable. Beneath the first, and last wooden panels were cylinders. There was an inclining mechanism to hold the ladder off the ground. At the top and bottom were two ropes on each side, and they were attached to the different cylinders. In the middle, serving as the fifth panel, was another pipe linked to those ropes. Finally, it was all connected to a lever that worked with a ratchet mechanism.

Caldwell looked down, before his eyes slowly shut, *"Pain is only a distraction. Keep your mouth locked no matter what,"* he thought to himself.

The room was dark, all the lights were off except those used for the Decoder. But the spotlight was fixed on what used to be known as a nightmare on Earth. The General introduced the device as, "The Rack. A medieval torture device, very effective during interrogations. Did you know its first recorded use in human history was from Ancient Greece?"

*"How does he know human history? It has all been destroyed, and only known to have been kept in the past, but it has already been altered...only two dimensions have remained unaffected, and only one is said to have been gifted with the Grey gene. He cannot know...please, heaven, he cannot tell."* Caldwell grimaced as thoughts raced through his head.

Ever since Caldwell had joined Liberty's military, he had been reading one of the oldest books of all and had discovered a form of strength within it. He held most precious one sentence that he kept with him as if to help himself find hope for his own soul, "Let him who is without sin cast the first stone." He whispered it to himself in confidence with the knowledge that everyone commits mistakes. That sentence alone helped him forgive himself from his past decisions. No one is without a stain.

Caldwell was placed on the rack. His hands were untied, and as he tried his best to move away, giving all, he had to move from the device, he was held by four large, and imposing Rakes. His wrists, despite all of the strength in his arms were tied, spread apart from his head. Then, his ankles were fastened by ropes below.

"It might be quite primitive, but I'm sure it is still extremely effective. Let's try a demonstration, shall we?"

The man wore a metallic mouthguard over his face. It went from below the upper side of his nose, and down his chin. The skin below his earlobes had started to grow over it, letting Caldwell know that it was permanently attached to his jaw.

"What are you hiding below your mask, Zachariah, hasn't it healed yet?" Caldwell sneered, his head turned Zachariah's way. Ash Zachariah was a Rake that he used to outrank in his home planet's military. Just by the way his eyes looked down at him, and the way Zachariah's head moved to stare at Caldwell, he knew. "So, you are infected."

The lever moved, and Caldwell felt the rope tensing as his arms and legs were being stretched. Zachariah reminded him that he was the one asking the questions as he slapped Caldwell with the back of his hand. He was wearing a glove with a pointy metal plate attached to it called, The Jaw-Breaker. Caldwell felt as if a rock had struck his cheekbone, and his head violently turned to the other side, blood coming out of his nose, and the corner of his mouth.

Both arms placed on each side of Caldwell's chest, Zachariah lowered himself inches away from his face. His one good eye fixed him, while the other had a deep scar from his forehead down his cheek. Caldwell, remembered carving the letter P for pirate, leaving Zachariah's eye to be blind, and entirely white with a grey ghost iris.

"You think you're the only one after Frank N. Stein?" He asked, his eyes squinting, his brows touching in the middle as it lowered, he added, "I've been in contact with her for several years before you found her life sign. I have spent the last decade right by her side working with her, and now that I have lost her, I'll stop at nothing to have her again." He straightened himself up, and moved his arm, letting the Rake know to move the lever again.

It was becoming harder to breathe. Caldwell tried to contract his muscles, but he couldn't move. "You're just a pitiful sorry excuse of a meat bag. You have failed as a General, and you failed as a human. The only good you can do the Milky Way is by letting yourself die, and pray that hell will let you in, because if I were the devil, I'd just let you fucking starve for eternity at my door." Zachariah looked away, "We both know that none of us are going to heaven one way or the other... not after the genocide you attempted on our own home world, and not after I stole the Vital virus."

Caldwell lifted his head, and shouted with a rough superior voice, "We both know I fired the dark matter bomb on Ares to stop our kind from taking over the Dome, and heading for other quadrants! I did it to save the galaxy from ourselves! Look at them for fuck's sake!"

He moved his head quickly to point at the Rake holding the lever, and saw him moving it again. The gruesome being stretched the ropes again. It had an empty, but loud popping sound, and Caldwell's cartilage around his shoulders, and hips were dislocated. He felt warmth spreading through his member, and muscles. Breathing was scarce, and oxygen was coming hard in between shallow breaths.

His voice was now only a shadow of what it had been, and blood coming up his face as he felt it warming. "You may kill me if it pleases you, but make sure you do it for the right reason, Ash." Caldwell felt the lever moving. His elbows, knees, and spine stretched to their limitations. There was only flesh holding his body together, and Caldwell almost lost consciousness. He felt the cascade of joints being estranged, ligaments and bones were all loose. His muscles were now entirely unresponsive. He felt his entire skin at the limit of tearing, like an elastic band about to snap. Caldwell would split open, and his abdominal wall would rip open leaving his organs to fall one after the other from below his ribcage.

"Why did you leave Frank N. Stein if you had her?" Long pauses in between each word, Caldwell tried to keep himself awake as his oxygen level was lowering, but people like him were able to endure pain very well, despite his human appearance.

"We loved each other, Jason. I was sent to find her, make sure she had the right genetic code, and report to my superiors." Zachariah's eyes closed, "I didn't think that I'd fall for a human woman. There's nothing backwards about the 21$^{st}$ century, you know, we still kill and envy others. Nothing has really changed." Caldwell thought him to be a little too philosophical, and his ex-Commander said, "My hair was a lot shorter, one of the Dome's doctors corrected my face and got rid of all the scars. I went to CaldTech Industries and was hired as an A.I. Specialist. I worked with her day after day, and for a decade we were so happy. I taught her martial arts, shooting, newer technologies…she taught me to love, to live."

Caldwell wondered about this Frank N. Stein. A few months ago, he thought it was a he, but then learned she was a woman. He knew Zachariah, he was a very intellectual male and not one to lower his guards easily. "I reported that she didn't have the good genetic code. I had to leave to protect her. That's how we broke up. I left." Were those tears on his face? "A few weeks afterwards, the Dome caught a plasma signal you had left behind and realized I lied. I was brought in the questioning room at the Dome's HQ and an Ensian doctor, the one you had the pleasure to meet, infected me with the very Vital virus I stole from our home planet."

"Why?" Caldwell asked, his voice choked by his own agony.

"Because I blocked my own memories from the hand device. I would never sell Frank's life, home, or love. If my life meant to be sacrificed to keep her safe, I'd do it and I did."

Caldwell had a hard time believing one of his own planet, Zachariah of all people, protected Frankie from the good will of his heart. He asked why the Dome was after Frank N. Stein and why now the Rakes were allied with them.

"For the same reason the Alliance is after her. They all want to use her to power their engines, because they believe that's what she was meant to be, a power source to travel faster than FTL. Do you see the bigger picture now, Jason?" Zachariah's eyes were filled with tears, "The Dome wants to enslave the galaxy before anyone can stop them. The Alliance is nothing more than hypocrites because I do know for a fact that they want Frank to replicate her genetics and create meta humans." Then he took a deep breath, "Us Rakes, you know why we allied ourselves with them...we want to take them down and take over...that's what organic beings do, Jason...we eat before getting eaten. It's a game of survival."

---

Frankie stared into Caldwell's eyes. He seemed lost in a thought. He stopped talking about his torture as if to keep some information from her. There was so much he wouldn't say. However, she could breathe easier now that she knew Caldwell wanted to know who the humanoid silhouette was, as it turned out to have been his torturer. She held his hand, but he still seemed far away in his mind.

"You came back with the tablet that you threw at my feet, and challenged me. When you wiped your nose dripping in blood, and said, 'I came. I saw. I conquered.' You proved to me that being strong isn't about how much blood you draw, but how much you spare."

Caldwell's eyes were hidden by tears when he looked at the Decoder. He suddenly fell to his knees and held Frankie by the hips. He wrapped his arms so tightly around her, that she felt her own heart sinking in her chest as she looked down at him, broken, and frail.

"I tried to go on with my life as if I had never been tortured. I drugged myself, but it only left me half asleep. I prayed for all of it to be gone, but I just ended up begging to enter hell, but knowing that it would reject me...they all did." His words were hidden by the cries that left his body moving in her arms. Frankie listened, caressed his head, and kept looking down as Caldwell fixed his eyes on the middle of the Decoder where he had been stretched, to what extent she didn't know, and would never dare to ask. "He broke me...after two days...he broke me."

He lifted his head, and looked into Frankie's eyes, who saw his irises switching from a frosty stare to a bright sapphire blue. She held his face in her palms, and said, "Someone saved you."

"Yes...it was you."

0500 Hours, 04th of October 2506 (
Gregorian calendar,)
Milky Way Galaxy, Orion Constellation, Pluto *Slicer*, Cargo 05.
Invasion: Day 12.
Ship status: Sustainable.
Loss: 32.

"Nothing begins. Nothing ends."

Frankie walked into the cargo area, and walked toward the Rake holding the lever. She ignored the tall half blind man, and with a swift and fast move, she plunged her hand inside the creature's belly below its ribcage. She moved her arm inside the creature reaching for its heart. She pulled it out, her arm drenched in the blood of the Rake. The heart pumped one last beat before becoming inert as she showed it to the Rake's face, and repeated with a dominant voice, "Nothing begins. Nothing ends."

She walked toward the tall man, and as she handed him the heart of his minion, she said, "Leave now."

The one memory she couldn't remember, the one scene she forgot, was how she first walked onto the ship. Frankie wanted to know how the memory could be activated, but instead, she caressed Caldwell's face. Both of his arms were still around her, holding onto her. For a moment, she felt as if he wished he had never fallen to his knees, so she reminded him, "I heard you snore."

His forehead was pressed against her breasts, and she held him against her as she slowly moved down to her knees. She made him look in her eyes, and reminded him, "I said there was only one Captain in the galaxy that I would follow, and that is you…only you."

Frankie moved forward, and their foreheads touched, their bodies melded a little closer, and their noses came in contact. She felt his warmth as her hands still caressed his cheeks, and the side of his jaw. His hands were now slowly moving up to her shoulders. Frankie felt him tilting his head, and his thin upper lip touched her own. His mouth partially opened, and she surrendered as he felt him softly pressing his lips against her own. She yielded to him like she had always wanted to.

Her left hand was moving down below the back of his neck, while her right hand was moving through his short black hair. She pressed her breasts against his chest as he forcefully pulled her toward him. His lips against hers, she felt his movement being just as dominant as his commanding personality. But then he pulled back for just a moment, and she half opened her eyes to see his lips, but lifted up her gaze to meet his own as he said with a breathy, but low voice, "Be mine." She nodded, "Will you?" She felt his head moving up and down, and his lips were on hers again, but suddenly he stopped and said, "I was yours the moment you came on board…forever will be."

He softly moved his arms down, his hands now grabbing onto her thighs, and moved her onto his lap. She felt him trying to get up. Frankie crossed her legs behind his back, and he lifted her and moved her to the Decoder where he tenderly laid her down. Frankie feared he might remember what had happened, but he said, "Let's make a new memory in this place."

His kiss stopped as he slowly straightened himself up. With a cocky, cornered smile he started lifting his grey shirt, and Frankie knew he noticed her glance at his very prominent swollen manhood. She bit her lip, and he winked at her. He threw his military shirt away. Frankie could finally see his bare muscular chest. It had a very fine layer of straight dark hair on the inner sides of his pectorals that stopped at the beginning of his ribcage. It left his well-defined abdominals nude, with a fine hairline starting below his navel going down underneath. Caldwell untied his pants, and Frankie lifted herself up, suddenly worried.

There was a broad white scar crossing from below his ribcage on one side and running to the other side. Frankie touched the scar with the tip of her fingers. She noticed another one underneath near his crotch. She moved on her knees, and with her hands, lifted his arms up. Caldwell obeyed, without a word. He stood in silence as Frankie inspected both lacerations from his elbows going up to his armpits, and then heading toward the back. On his chest were spots of branding burns. *You fell to pieces. The rack stretched you to pieces.*

Frankie moved toward him, kissing with her blossom peach lips each of his burns, and slowly moved toward his neck, softly caressing each piece of hurt flesh. She moved to his jaw, right below his little-honeyed lips, and finally, he lowered his head. When she felt the tip of his tongue teasing her upper lip, she let him in.

She felt his need to be in possession of her. He wanted to show her that he was a strong, and powerful man. Frankie let him tenderly lie her down. She wrapped her arms around him, as he moved his kiss to her ear, and whispered, "You're mine." She answered, "So are you." She turned her attention to him, he grinned, and said, "Forever will be." He finished untying the string of his jogging pants, and took them off. Frankie began to undress as well.

"Computer. Seal the cargo bay doors. Permission Alpha A1."

"Captain Caldwell, voice identification recognized. Doors are sealed."

Frankie could tell by his crotch that he was longing for her, as he said with a breathless voice, "You don't know how long I've been waiting for this." He added, "I have dreamed of this moment." Frankie had been fantasizing of this instant for so long, she wondered if she could last as long as he could once she finally felt his skin against her own.

Wearing her white cotton underwear with a trim of lace at the top, she thought to herself, *Not very sexy, Frankie*. The way he looked at her, his deep blue eyes, and his hungry smile, now without any pretense, she wished she could know what went through his mind as he pulled her sports bra over her head. A little shy, she moved her arms to hide her breasts, although generous, she felt embarrassed as she was not as 'runway model' shaped as he was. But Caldwell held her closer. As he kissed her neck, near her ear, she felt the tip of his teeth. On her lobe he whispered, "You're just as beautiful as I imagined."

She rubbed her head against his, and he moved his hand up to her breast. Just by his firm grip she knew he was confident of his every movement, as she was shy. She worried she might not be as experienced as he was. His hand was slowly moving down, and she was about to close her legs, again a little timid, but he began caressing the inside of her thigh with the back of his index finger near her underwear. Her legs were not entirely closed, but Caldwell kept teasing her, patiently until she opened her eyes and saw his grin. She whispered, "I want you."

He stopped, and removed his hand. Frankie lifted herself up leaning on her elbow, and asked, "Why are you stopping when you know I want you." He lifted his eyebrows, and had a satisfied smile as he lay on his back, "You played hard to get, why shouldn't I?" Frankie knew better, he said he had dreamed about the moment their skin would rub one against the other, and she would make it come true.

Frankie rolled on her side, so one of Caldwell's legs was in between hers. Her vagina against his thigh, she saw his manhood reacting to her warm touch. She looked into his eyes, he smiled, "What are you doing?"

Her fingers played near his manhood, and she said, "You'd do anything for me." She then touched him gently over his underwear, moving lower between his legs, her hand with a confident gesture, just hard enough that she could see him taking deeper breaths, his eyes rolled, and she said, "You promised." His arm over his forehead, she caressed his swollen desirable organ.

"Anything." He moaned, "I would do anything for you."

"Take me."

He instantly shifted her beneath him, and spread her legs confidently, but his touch was the softest she had ever felt. He took off his fitted underwear, and tore hers off with one movement. She looked at him, strong, manly, and she knew he needed to be the Alpha. Frankie couldn't wait to finally feel him deep, and hard within her. Caldwell leaned over, her legs wrapped around him, and she pulled him toward her, but then she felt his fingers reaching down. He slowly slid a couple inside, caressing her clitoris with his index, and major finger, effortlessly moving around as she's been ready for him since the moment she crossed his gaze.

Her eyes closed, and she felt his lips on her own, kissing her again and again.

Teasing her only with the tip of his finger at her opening, she already felt on edge, and she arched her back releasing a soft moan. He removed his hand, and finally, she felt his manhood against her, hard as a rock, big, and swollen. As he slid in she released a loud cry as he lifted himself onto his elbows. She dug her fingers into his back. His perfectly muscular organ moved back and forth at a pace that had her on the edge of ecstasy. She felt a burst of warmth, like a fire igniting and spreading through her entire body.

Caldwell slowed down, and pulled away, leaving only the head to caress her vagina. She felt him, still inside, and wanting nothing more, but for him to reach the deepest he could. She clung onto him. He lay on top of her, her breasts pressing against his chest, and she then felt him sliding in again. Frankie wanted him, and as his rhythm changed, she found herself craving more. "Harder," she moaned. His movements roughened, and she could barely hold any longer, when she heard subtle growls from him. Feeling his lower, fine layer of hair rubbing against her, making it even better, again, another flash of warmth spread through her, and she tried to move her hips closer to his. He quickened, and hardened his rocking movements, rapid, faster, rougher, and harder, she released a cascade of moaning as her back arched, and her mouth opened. His arms were holding onto her, she heard his growl, and then a soft release from his muscles relaxing.

Caldwell softly caressed her face as she moved from her arched position. She wondered what would happen now that he had made her his. He moved in closer, and kissed her again, one last movement of his manhood reaching deep within, her eyes rolled back, and then she felt him softly pulling away. She looked at him, he was a little sweaty, and she thought he was even more irresistible after this intimate relation, finally coming true for Frankie who now felt entirely lost.

As long as they had not shared their bodies, he was the one winking at her, and softly smiling. But now, she didn't know what would happen between them. She reached for her sports bra, and put it on, her yoga pants followed, and she felt Caldwell's kiss on the back of her shoulder. She heard him reaching for his own clothes, and when dressed, she turned around to face him. Frankie saw him place himself, he glanced sideways at her and then turned his head toward her. She felt her cheeks warming. "You can look all you want. You don't have to be shy or discreet about it."

Once dressed, Caldwell helped Frankie up, and they both walked toward the exit. Suddenly Frankie feared going back to her quarters. She wondered what would happen to her if she did. When the doors opened, and they arrived on the personal quarterdeck, she was about to turn left, he grabbed her by her waist, "Where are you going, my quarters are that way."

She followed Caldwell to his personal room, and she thought he would've let go of her as other members of the crew walked past them, but he held on to her hand. At his quarters, the doors opened, and Frankie stepped inside. It was the first time she had actually stood in Caldwell's room and it had a subtle, enchanting resinous smell.

The room was dark, his walls painted black. He had a solid table with two sofas as chairs. On Frankie's left was a desk with a monitor screen, and other office related objects, such as a second screen, and tablets. It faced the glass wall exposing space to almost the entire room. At the end of the corridor, behind the desk was his bathroom. On the right, was his queen-sized bed with black sheets, well displayed, and she wondered if he made the bed himself. The bed, contrarily to Frankie, had the headboard against one of the black walls as his quarters were shaped loosely like the letter J, so the bed faced space. Above it was a reproduction of a painting of Leonardo da Vinci's 'An Angel in Green with a Vielle.'

Frankie stood in the middle of Caldwell's quarters taking everything in. When she heard him speak, she jumped. "Now that we've slept together are you going to play harder to get?" She smiled, but kept to herself, "Frankie, it's me, Jason. You just saw me naked." She chuckled, but admitted that she had never slept with someone, and just left it at that. Her last relationship had lasted for a decade. One night stands weren't her style.

"See, I wanted you so badly that I let it happen, and now, I'm regretting it." She looked away embarrassed, "I'm not that kind of woman, I guess."

"Who said I was that kind of man?" He shrugged, and with his hands apart rectified,

"Well, not anymore. I mean, it's good to be Captain. Then again, I'm over that age."

Frankie grabbed his hand as he was about to reach for his cooler door, which was built in the wall. Caldwell stopped, and looked at her, suddenly worried as she asked, "What are we Jason?" Frankie asked, "What do you mean?" His face softened, and a smile appeared, "I meant it when I said that you were mine. Moreover, I meant for a long while. Remember, I said forever?"

Frankie stepped back. She could understand the confusion on Caldwell's face. After all, she just admitted to not being the kind of woman to sleep with a man, and then forget about it. He confirmed that he wanted to be with her, and yet, she moved away. He faced her, his head tilted to the side, and asked what was wrong. Frankie hugged herself, and said, "I'm a ufologist, I worked at CaldTech Industries for ten years, and went out with my superior."

# CHOOSE YOUR LIE

The next day, Frankie worked with Dr. Gillman on trying to figure out the Rake's gene that was restructuring King's DNA. After what she had learned about the memory from the Captain, which she kept to herself, Frankie thought she might have had a theory. Looking at the scans, and DNA structure of Commander King, Frankie had both her hands on each side of the tablet. She leaned to support her upper body over the table, and said "What if the Rakes are trying to copy the Greys to come back to their original appearance?"

"What do you mean?" Dr. Gillman asked holding another tablet synced with Frankie's.

"I mean, what if there are two Rake's species. One that somehow devolved to what we know the Rakes to look like now, and one that remained the same, like

General Zachariah?"

"Are you saying that this might be a virus disguised as a mutated gene?"

"Yes."

Frankie might not have been a biotechnologist or a scientist, but she did have an acute sense of deduction. Frankie couldn't go one day without thinking about King, and feeling a massive weight of guilt on her shoulders. It was time for her to do something with that Grey gene of hers that seemed to be triggered every time she was in danger, or when the ship wanted to let her know something.

Caldwell walked in the room the moment Frankie asked, "Doctor, were you onboard the *Slicer* when the Rakes invaded the ship for twelve days?"

Suddenly, the doctor seemed quite uncomfortable as she tried to hold her tablet higher, hiding a side of her face. Her claws dug into the translucent tablet, and. Frankie could tell she was hiding something. Frankie explained that their uniform had changed. There was a different crew on board Slicer and somehow the ship was communicating with her by sharing information through a telepathic link.

"Doctor, if I'm here to help I need to know who I'm helping and by who, I mean what species. The ship is transmitting information to me. It wants me to know something about the crew. What is it?"

"We were boarded many times."

"Tell me something I don't know. Like, you've known our Captain for two decades and hide his psychological profile. Why did the ship want me to know that about him?"

"Maybe to reassure you that you are not alone going through psychological distress."

"Or that he has been Captain from the beginning? He jumped from military school to the big chair, just like that?"

Dr. Gillman ordered her nurses, and staff to go to the other section of the medical facility. She ordered them to stay on the other side and ordered the doors to close. Frankie had all intentions of saving King, but without the truth, she couldn't trust anyone with his life, except her own hands and she wasn't a doctor.

"Frankie, listen to me." Dr. Gillman begged as she put her tablet down,

"Whatever it is you want to know about Captain Caldwell, is not my truth to tell."

Frankie glanced at the man she had slept with the night before, and he had his arms crossed over his chest. He had a glow to his skin that made her wonder if it was because of the night they spent together making love over and over again. She could almost relive their passion as he walked forward, "This ship is not LSS. It's mine."

Frankie gasped, "What do you mean?"

"It means I came here with my own ship and struck a deal with high Liberty Intel to have a false human identity in exchange for my ship. I was reduced from General to Captain and that's why Dr. Gillman could only write Captain in her personal logs' entries...in Liberty's files I have a made-up career."

"What about the uniforms?" Frankie asked Caldwell, finally spitting out some truth, as she stared at him with a severe look.

"Some people tagged along my journey from my home planet to Liberty. The only uniforms I had were from my planet's military. When I arrived, Liberty's Intel accepted my deal on the spot, and we were sent into deep space to fight. We had no time for uniforms and regulations. They just gave me a crew. It was after a month or two that I was sent to outposts to receive new uniforms and the book on the 'Alliance's Ways' bullshit."

Frankie couldn't understand how the enemy wouldn't recognize the ship being from the enemy's world. "How could you hide your ship?"

"Those are highly sophisticated holoprojectors. On the outside she looks like one of their 'Icefall' line ship in the shape of an icicle, when in reality..." Caldwell closed the area around the main medical computer and after the system recognized his hand print, he projected his ship, "... she looks like a cleaver like you saw before."

Frankie looked at the hieroglyph and made the remark that other than the Greys, no other species could recognize the symbol. Caldwell justified, "I said it was from my home world. I didn't say it belonged to it. This ship was in one of the military hangars, just like your Area 51 where they keep little green men."

"All right," Frankie said while staring at the holographic projection of the real *Slicer*. Now that she knew more about Caldwell and trusted his story, she focused on the hieroglyph. It saw its share of battle, she almost mistook the design as a Viking letter until she felt her eyes contracting to fix on the name of the ship, "PLL – RA – A."

"What does that stand for?"

"All I can say is that this ship belonged to the Greys." Frankie saw Caldwell's eyes widening as his brows lifted, so did Dr. Gillman. They both asked how she drew her conclusion and again, Frankie would prove her deduction to be superior to many.

"RA."

Frankie zoomed on the hieroglyph and explained that so far, while the Alliance used Ancient Greece as a point of reference for their people, the Greys seemed quite obsessed with Ancient Egypt. They had their own system. The Rakes tried to crack it, but hieroglyphs from Ancient Egypt could reveal itself to be quite complex without a background in history and most precisely, Egyptology.

"The Greys never left clues behind. It's their codex that was scattered and I bet that codex was about how this ship in particular works. All I've been translating so far were instructions, Alaska even had suspicions about the ship. She knew it wasn't LSS."

Frankie stared at Caldwell, he knew about Alaska's suspicions, and he had confessed wanting to let her know but feared the secret would spread. Frankie agreed he made the right move if uncertain of Alaska's loyalty to keeping a secret to herself, but assured him she could. "Ra means, Ruler of the Sun. He is the leader of Ancient Egypt's mythology."

"It is no secret that due to this temporal war, Earth's ancient history had been altered time and time again. You are the only one capable of retrieving more information on...*Ra*." Caldwell said with a stern look while looking at Dr. Gillman, "This ship has an organic entity. We do not know where it is or if it is still active. We lost our previous translator to the war."

Frankie nodded, she understood her place in the war. She had to reshape *Ra* to its original function. She lifted her eyes and saw the pod. King was still floating in the artificial amniotic liquid. She had promised herself that she would save him, and she would.

"Let's move to the war room," Caldwell said, erasing all traces of his file before releasing the medical room and walking away. They went to a deck that only Caldwell's most trustful crew had access to. He chose his senior crew by their expertise, and usefulness to a mission. However, Frankie knew he continued to keep a secret from his entire crew.

As they gathered around the monitor table shaped like a diamond, at its point was Captain Caldwell. On his right should have been his tactical officer, King, but the place was empty for now. On his left was the linguistic specialist, Draca Wolf, who acquired the knowledge of various alien languages unknown to the Alliance. Across from Wolf was Helle Madsen, his most trusted sniper. At the opposite end was Frankie, who became not only the Grey specialist, but his first in command as of that moment when mentioning it to the official log and entry, while Alaska Leclerc stood at her side as the chief engineer, and now second in command.

Normally, there would be another officer beside Helle, but they had lost so many that the commanding crew decided to leave it empty. Caldwell didn't trust that many people. Cadet Zwally could've replaced one of the five original main crew members, but she rarely left the ship. She had to be at her post and prepared for surprise attacks. Over the years, even Captain Caldwell couldn't stop the killing of his military officers. Now, stuck in Rake Space, Frankie hoped they would find a way to map a safe route out of there.

Frankie took the place of one of the five officers they had lost. Another one was Dr. Omeo Watson, the psychiatrist on the ship, but he normally was not present because of Frankie's arachnophobia. His appearance was too familiar to the eight-legged arachnid.

"Join us, Dr. Watson," The Captain said as he welcomed him to the table. Helle moved to be on Frankie's right side, and so the psychiatrist, who had studied the behavior of the Rakes for the past four years, joined the main senior crew of the *Slicer*.

"This ship's name is not *Slicer*." Caldwell had both his hands on the monitor screen showing the falcon head shape of the ship's true nature. A holographic projection showed its origin paint, and side where the name was displayed. His head looking down, his eyes moved to meet Frankie's gaze who hugged herself, and felt her hands shaking with the presence of Watson. She stared at Caldwell who winked at her with a subtle grin as the wrinkles on his forehead carved in, reminding her that he was the man of her dreams. She calmed down.

"What do you mean?" Helle asked, her bright red hair tied up, her bright blue eyes fixed on the Captain.

"My first officer, Stein will answer." He answered.

Frankie took a deep breath. She tried to remember all the science fiction shows she had watched in the past. It had to help her take command of a team she had known as her friends for over the past four years. She closed her eyes, relaxed, and felt Alaska's hand grabbing her fingers, and give a good shake as if to let her know, "You got this."

Frankie pointed at the ship that appeared in the 3D holographic representation and showed the vessel from above. She informed the crew, "It has an Egyptian mythological animal looking shape." She enlarged the hieroglyphs on the top view of the vessel that demonstrated the exact same ones she had seen in the medical facility.

"The Greys have *Ra* as a representative symbol of themselves. Meaning, they obviously see their species as not only a superior one, but a guiding light." She then spoke of all the research she had done on the collection of Grey transcriptions, and findings, "I'm not an archaeologist, and the task was hard to accomplish. However, after my realization of their fascination with Ancient Egypt, I concluded that codex is an instruction manual on how to operate this very ship and most likely their most precious technology."

Caldwell had his arms crossed over his chest. Frankie had not yet decoded the entire manuscript. Reinforcing her theory, she mentioned da Vinci's codex back in the Renaissance era. It backed her hypothesis on the Greys' methodological way of thinking and proceeding, "Subliminal messages are effective." She suggested how the Grey's usage of ancient human mythology might have been a good way for them to protect their identity by hiding on Earth, a 'backward' species, from their knowledge. "Many on Earth associate the Greys to bad people, but when we look at history, so were scientists."

She looked back at her Captain, who now had all eyes fixed on him. He deviated their attention to Watson. The Anwanian was very slim, shorter than Caldwell, and had a russet skin color. The texture seems reminiscent of snakes with larger pores. His head was shaped like a reversed water drop, the tip pointing down to his chin. Needless to say, Watson was hairless, with eight eyes of different sizes adorning his head, permitting him to see all angles at all times. His nose was almost invisible, and his mouth had a wide opening, permitting both his mandibles to stick out. This allowed him to be better understood when speaking with a very unique voice, almost like white noise or bad radio signal tones.

He turned on his voice adapter. It was a gadget Alaska had come up with, and he used it to focus his vocal cords on one note at a time. It allowed him more freedom to practice his vocation among the crew that were not accustomed to this type of voice. "The Rakes have shown much interest in the Greys. Their reason is unknown to this day, and there is nothing but speculation that I can provide. However, with the help of Commander Stein's recent discovery, I believe that they are after her."

Watson lifted his head, and pointed all around him, "You mean the ship?" Caldwell asked squinting his eyes and leaning on the monitor table again. The Anwanian nodded, "Yes. What if this mysterious codex is the manual to operate *Ra* to its full capacity as Frankie says? Would it be so far-fetched to believe this starship wasn't meant to operate on blubber, or that the specific cleaver...maybe somehow related to an Egyptian shape has an actual purpose, other than just looking like a weapon?"

Of course, everyone's curiosity was aroused. Wolf, Madsen, and the others started talking at the same time. Frankie stood aside. Her eyes were fixed on Caldwell who stared at the shape of the ship. His arms were back to being crossed on his chest, one hand up, picking at his bottom lip while remaining silent.

"What made you think of such a fascinating theory?" Madsen asked Watson. "Commander Stein's research. It actually gives their behavior an explanation I couldn't find before." Watson explained that time and time again, the *Slicer* would find traces of a specific ancient human radio frequency and follow it. It would guide them to the next piece of the puzzle that had been left by the Greys. Then, when the Rakes picked up on it, they would overpower them by beating them to the location almost instantly, "Why would they let us leave otherwise?"

All stayed silent until Alaska spoke up, "They know what this ship is capable of. They just don't know how to make the proper adjustments. We do the work, and then, they steal it from us."

Frankie still had her eyes on Caldwell. He was silent, and lost in his thoughts picking at his lips. She knew him too well by now. He was hiding something from his trusted crew. Something was up, but she couldn't tell what. Somehow, the words of Commander King surfaced in her mind like a warning, "Do not trust him. He is a lie." She couldn't help it, like a moth to a flame, she would burn again.

"How do we beat the Rakes?" Wolf asked looking at Madsen. "The question is, how do we know we have all the pieces of the codex?" Alaska added, "If there is another way to make the *Slicer* work, I want to know. Because the longer we stay in Rake Space, the more we grow like a giant target, especially if they are after this ship!" Then, Madsen said, "What if they know Frankie's our translator?"

Everyone stared at Frankie, and she saw Caldwell letting go of his lip. Slowly his arms bent down to both sides of his body. She stared at him, a light veil of tears covering her eyes as she shyly smiled. "Captain?" She asked with a broken voice.

Caldwell, without any hesitation, slid a piece of paper toward Alaska, who picked it up, and looked at it. Frankie had her eyes fixed on Caldwell the entire time. His eyes never lost hers. Both without a smile, both had either too many emotions to process or not enough. Frankie felt afraid, and knew Caldwell was hiding something.

"This...it's...it can't."

Frankie's gaze clung to Caldwell's as he spat out more lies, staring back into the bright green of her hazel eyes. "It's the recipe for Binary Core. It will efficiently contain the fuel needed for the ship. The Rakes had the fuel, but not the codex to understand how to operate what *Ra* was meant to do."

Then she heard Madsen's voice before he added more lies, "Which is what, Captain?"

"Re-establishing the original timeline that has been tampered with for centuries."

"How do you know, Sir?" Wolf asked the Captain as he shrugged, everyone unaware that Caldwell was about to lie yet again, except Frankie, "Secret intel."

# THE MODERN PROMETHEUS

Frankie got off duty after the war room meeting that lasted for hours, and she thought it was now time for her to take a shower. She needed to and try to erase the thought of...Caldwell's lies, as she could recognize them so easily. He was hiding, and she didn't know why, but she knew she had no rights to force the truth out of him because she too, was hiding the truth from everyone on the ship.

She walked to her bathroom hidden on the right side of her quarters. When the light turned on, Frankie reduced the luminosity to twenty percent, and turned on the water to her heat preferences, very enduring to warmth. She removed her clothing and stepped inside the glass rectangle. The three-hundred-and-sixty-degree water jets sprayed water all around her. Frankie took her bottle of strawberry shower gel and scrubbed herself before washing her hair.

She couldn't help but think about Caldwell's almond eyes, his mature gaze, and irresistible large, and strong hands caressing her skin. Flashes of his grip on her denuded hips, when pulling her toward him, his manhood hard, and big moving back, and forth in rhythm with his desire of pleasuring her, she could still hear his groan, and breathing. It made her suddenly weak, and she bit her lip while the water rinsed off all residual strawberry soap. Her hand was about to reach her most intimate organ...then, the war room surfaced, and she expressed herself aloud.

"Why did you lie, Jason? I don't know what the truth is behind the Binary Core, but I know you lied to us, and more importantly, to me. There's this something about you that acts as an enticement on me. I'm attracted to you like iron to a magnet."

"Quite a romantic analogy, careful you're making me hot."

That wasn't Caldwell's voice. She recognized the silvery tone covered in honey instantly. Frankie quickly ordered all lights to turn off. In the pitch-black environment, Frankie silently walked out of the shower, and wrapped a towel around herself. She grabbed her underwear, and a bralette, and put them on. Her keen senses on high alert, she reached for her razor, still wet after the shower.

*How did Zachariah get on Ra? There's no way he could've bypassed the security system that Alaska, and I reworked together after what happened to Nakamo.*

"Frankie, I need to talk with you."

The door opened and let in a faint light from the corridor in night mode. Frankie recognized Caldwell's voice, and wished he hadn't, just walked in to her quarters. Then, there was no more sound. Frankie deduced Caldwell understood something was wrong, and that there was an intruder in her quarters. Caldwell could have called for security, but he was smarter than that. He knew the presence might have been essential or at least, Frankie deducted that much by the way all fell quiet.

"So, you both fucked. Wow, it only took what, four years and eight months, give or take?" Frankie was not about to feel ashamed or enraged by his comment until, "Too bad, I wished I would've been your only alien. My cock is more impressive than his. You can at least agree to that, Frank!" A roll of her eyes, and Frankie silently crawled along the exterior wall of her bathroom to reach the living area. "I only saw your body under the water through the vapor. Caldwell, you lucky bastard. She only had one man before you, and after more than four years, it must've been tight, and gratifying to get in knowing how wet she becomes just thinking of you."

It was apparent that Zachariah wanted a reaction from them. He wanted to know where they were. "PBU!" Frankie said aloud by mistake. Instantly, she knew Zachariah had pinpointed her position. She tried to walk away, but felt a grip on her head, and a hand over her mouth. "Lights on!" Caldwell shouted.

Zachariah was holding Frankie tight against his chest. Her head now tilted back, a blade was pressing against her throat. She said, "You're not going to kill or endanger me. I'm too valuable to you alive." The alien nodded and admitted she was right. Then his hand moved over her right breast, and as he closed his hand on her, Frankie had tears rolling down her face. Suddenly she heard a low growl coming from Caldwell and his irises were covered in deep blue with what seemed to be stars.

"Look at your precious Jason. Don't you see what King was trying to warn you about? Walrians are not known to have changing irises. Is your vagina blinding your common sense? He's no Walrian!" Zachariah sneered.

Frankie knew having stars on irises that previously changed color from a human blue eye color to a deep ocean one wasn't a Walrian trait. She also knew he wasn't part of the species he claimed to be a part of because she saw the memory of the ship. Caldwell never did anything to hurt his crew, the ship, or Frankie. He might have followed the primary mission of *Slicer* but never had he voluntarily endangered the ship. Frankie was not about to give up on him.

"Let her go." Caldwell growled.

"You're in no position for bargaining. Besides, she was mine before she was yours. Ten years we've been together." Zachariah's nose was deep in Frankie's hair, and Caldwell added, "You have no shame, hiding behind a woman to protect yourself? You are more of a coward than I remember!"

Zachariah violently pushed Frankie out of his way. She jumped back on him from behind. Both her hands locked around his throat, and Zachariah fell on top of her. Frankie skillfully moved to the side, grabbing onto his arm, and locked it with her legs to break it. Caldwell jumped on top of Zachariah, and pounded on his chest as he roared in his face, "Touch one hair on Frankie's head again, and I'll decimate your entire fucking shit race!"

Suddenly, the body disappeared in a swirl of green particles. "Portable Beaming Unit, I knew it. But how did I know it?" Frankie said gasping for air. "What's going on?" She asked, grasping her head, everything was coming alive within her mind. She held onto her head, as she felt Caldwell's grip on her as he pulled her body toward him. Frankie wrapped her arms around him, and felt a sharp sting from the back of her head, like a bee sting. It penetrated through her skull, and slowly pierced through her brain, and came out between her eyes. The sensation was almost unbearable, almost.

Her voice, monotonous and without emotion, Frankie fixed empty space and like a voicemail she opened her mouth and words fell from her lips.

"We have long studied your kind. Humans were the perfect recipients for our knowledge. They were young enough to learn, and child-like enough to impress. Our species is dying, but we wished for our data to prosper. Despite finding the perfect race to carry our DNA, hold our species history, and technological advancements, we have found that not all of you were ready to use it in good faith. Many were too young."

The message continued...

"Sadly, humans were the only compatible species. After millennia of fascination with your species we were, somehow, pleased. Then, our enemies broke the space-time continuum, and had us hasten the examinations of the human race. As a last hope, we found you. You would become our vehicle to all we know. In time, our genes would merge, and your DNA would become your greatest asset in the war to come. Understand, we have not envisaged our shared information to create this inconvenience. However, you have to protect yourself at all costs. If you hear this message, our beloved Frankenstein, know that all is now unlocked. You are now capable of more than you can imagine. Be wise, be kind, and most of all, be courageous. You are our star child."

The message ended, and the sting disappeared. Frankie's eyes were covered in bloody tears by the pain the sting inflicted on her. Blood came out from her ears, nose, mouth and tear glands. She asked Caldwell what happened, because she did remember the message, but not speaking it aloud for all to hear. She looked around and recognized Alaska, Wolf, Madsen, Dr. Gillman, and Dr. Watson. Her eyes, back on Caldwell who held her hand, said, "You actually repeated the message six times before you gained your senses back. I called them, because I thought maybe they could help. I wanted Dr. Gillman here to supervise you and she noticed your brain activity increasing. There was, of course, other medical gibberish that basically means you're at full Grey capacity."

"I guess that explains why I never felt I belonged on Earth." She chuckled, trying to keep calm. She wiped her nose and sat down on her bed before Dr. Gillman approached her with a sanitized wipe to clean her face. Frankie rested her right arm on her knee, and said, "I thought I was just a vehicle for the Greys, but they called me their 'star child.' I guess I meant more to them than just a DNA storage unit. They admitted having a fascination with my species, which has me reconsider a few human sudden advancements." Frankie watched Captain Caldwell reached for the ergonomic chair and sat beside her, he held her hand and reinforced, "You obviously meant a lot to them. They thought Earth could protect you due to it being so young compared to the rest of us. The only way to explain how your existence came to us is that someone betrayed you, the Greys and the Alliance."

Frankie had to agree. There was no other possibility for her existence or at least the idea of a human, carrying the Grey's encoded DNA. So far, she had used some of the Grey's abilities, but Dr. Gillman was sure that she's been using it at full capacity. At this moment, Frankie knew that she had not been because the message revealed to be the triggering element of the full awakening of her given abilities by her 'star parents.'

A jump later, after noticing four eyelids blinking, she noticed Dr. Watson standing in the dark. The psychiatrist was aware of Frankie's condition, and always respected her space so she wouldn't have more anxiety. However, Caldwell stated that he thought this time he had to be present because of his detective work he had done on her throughout the time she had been aboard.

"We know the Greys just as much as humans do. They are a secretive race, and as far as we know, they might now be a 'were' and entirely extinct. The one they chose to be their legacy is you, Frankie. You are an artifact, a monument to their existence." Dr. Watson stayed hidden in the darkest corner of the room, only his voice could be heard by Frankie who felt a strong and gripping feeling surrounding her heart as tears built up in her eyes, "While many said humankind is a backward species, the Grey saw you as a child, who like any other, needed a parent. Sadly, not all humans could carry their genes and along came you, Frankie."

"You're saying that I'm the Modern Prometheus." She chuckled between tears falling down her cheeks. The task of defending what her 'star parents' gave her might have been too big for her to endure, but instead, she said, "It's okay. I was a hybrid from the very beginning. A black sheep if you will." She added, "Left handed, eyes that change color, double jointed, IQ above average, overly developed deduction and logic. Artistic yet incredibly neat...I'm a walking contradiction. I'm used to walking paths alone and being misunderstood." The moment she could feel her friends about to comfort her, she stood up, "Now, I don't have to walk alone anymore. Now, I'm among people who are different, because each of you are the most advanced of their own species. No one on *Ra* is alone."

Alaska stepped forward, handed her an electronic tablet and said, "Commander, I finished the analysis of the residual particles left behind by Zachariah. The results concluded with a perfect match to King's alterations from the Decoder room." Dr. Gillman nodded. "This means that your hypothesis on the fact that Rakes had two subspecies, one resembling human, and one devolving, and contagious like a virus is true." Frankie read the results, "What makes them contagious?" She looked at Caldwell, but he stayed silent.

"I'll go back to my lab and try to come up with a serum to stop the virus from spreading. We need to act soon before Nakamo reaches the point of no return." Dr. Gillman added, "I'll find a way, Commander, he's not alone. He has this whole crew behind him. Like you said, no one here on *Ra* is alone anymore."

All knew what to do, and the doors to her quarters slid open. As he was about to leave, Frankie grabbed Caldwell's arm. She saw him look down at her grip, his head forward, and guards staring at them. She fixed him with a stare as he looked up, his wrinkles carving into his forehead with a forced smile, he said, "I'm still on duty, Commander Stein." She answered, "No shit, Sir."

He walked back in, and the doors closed. He didn't seem amused and Frankie wasn't either. With a strong voice, Caldwell said, without elevating his voice, "Don't you ever do that in front of my officers again. If I show weakness before them because of you, it will affect the chain of command, and the distance I must keep for this crew to function properly. Am I clear?"

"Then why don't you tell them you're a Rake, and that's the reason you know the recipe to build a Binary Core to power this ship and that you might know how to cure Nakamo?"

Caldwell slouched, closed his eyes, and brought his index finger, and thumb to the side of the bridge of his nose, and rubbed the corners of his eyes. "I wondered how long it would take you to shove it in my face. I'm a fraud." Frankie looked down, "You should know better. I would never call you out in front of your crew. In my quarters, between you me alone, yes. Now, do you know how to cure Nakamo?"

"No. I was a physicist, not a medical scientist. However, I do know someone who would know. Zachariah was the leader in the biotechnology department."

"You scare me, you know. I'm terrified of your abilities, and skills, and yet, I...I can't say no to you."

Caldwell's hand came up to her cheek and caressed her face before he whispered with his grave, husky voice, "Don't be afraid of me. I would never hurt you, Frankie. You are the most beautiful being I have ever seen." All the information needed, her Grey DNA at full capacity, and hope to cure King in sight, Frankie only had one more question.

"Now tell me, how fucked are we if we stay in Rake Space?"

"More than you know." Caldwell grimaced.

Frankie understood there was no more time to waste, especially that Zachariah had proven himself to be extremely dangerous with the PBU at his disposition by the Dome. It was clear that he wanted them to know he would come back. There would be no way to know when he would beam onboard *Ra*. The look on Caldwell's face said it all as he was exhausted, and ashamed. She took his hand and led him to her bed

# A.D WAYNE

where he laid down. He was on duty, yet, never did he try to resist Frankie who contacted Alaska, "Take the con." Alaska answered, being a commander, "Yes, Sir."

Caldwell took off his official shirt and threw it as far away as he could from himself. Frankie watched him bring the base of his palms to his eyes, and rub them before he sighed. "Tell me, how was your life before this mess?" He asked Frankie, and she didn't want to answer, because she knew who he wanted her to talk about. It would bring him even more pressure to make it all perfect—well, as close as perfect. The past was the past.

"Why don't you talk to me about your hideout, and how you managed to enter the Alliance with a fake three-quarter human, one third Walrian hybrid fake story?"

"I knew Dr. Gillman. She's Reptilian. They have the ability of hypnosis. She basically met with the high council of the Alliance, and got me in. The file that you saw was the one she made for herself, not the Alliance. She only changed a few things, in the case of someone as smart, and nosy as you, would find out."

"Why both Human, and Walrian?"

Frankie was sitting on the side of her hip, her legs resting near Caldwell. Suddenly uncomfortable around him, she looked down at her own hands. He reached out and took her hands holding them tight.

"Ever since I discovered the human race, I felt as if I had found my own species again. The Rakes used to be like humans. We were proud, advancing at a quicker pace than yours, but not that much so to be arrogant about it. Then, we moved forward too fast. We discovered how to replicate and direct an artificially constructed, binary black hole. We launched into space and began the journey through our quadrant. At first, all was good...until we started to see the repercussions of using the engines. It caused my species to regress and devolve. The containment field wasn't strong enough, and slowly it was deconstructing everything surrounding it."

In the Scorpius Quadrant, the Rakes were the most dangerous species to encounter. Caldwell was an exception, and Frankie wasn't ready to give up on him, and kept listening to his story while he held on to her fingers as if to cope with the reality that kept on tearing his life apart. Rakes were dangerous, which meant Caldwell was too, but that night all Frankie saw was a man hoping to make things right.

"As much as I would love to be proud of my species, I am not. I also refused to let humans become Rakes. We have the same weaknesses, Frankie. Thirst for power over equality, arrogance over the pursuit of knowledge, corruption over justice. There is no perfect species, only perfect ideas of what it should be."

Caldwell was not a young man in his twenties, and his wisdom was showing through his words. He was an experienced man. However, Frankie knew that he was hiding something else that he would reveal in time.

"Of course, my true appearance is not as close to humans as you see it now. I was given three separated medications to forever change my appearance, what you see now. The only side effect is that my true irises would sometimes show, and it first came through when I...um." Caldwell cleared his throat, looked down at his chest, and looked at the ceiling again, "...had feelings for you. They changed from the pre-established light blue to a deeper shade of it."

To protect his little imperfections, Dr. Gillman decided to have him at less than thirty percent Walrian. It covered anything that could go wrong. However, now that Frankie knew she dared to ask, "You know right now, the ship could use someone like you to save its purpose, and maybe me in the process."

Caldwell turned on his side, and with a broad smile, said, "I know of a dimension that wasn't affected by this shit. We could move there, you and I, and live together as long as we are given." Of course, his happiness, and his joy brought a smile to Frankie. It made her feel like a monster reminding him, "Would you be able to live with the guilt of leaving nearly six hundred crewmates, your crew, behind to their fate? Would you be okay to leave them in Rake Space knowing that you might have been the key to end this war?"

On his back again, Frankie held his hand, brought it to her lips, and kissed it over and over again. She said, "Come what may, I will stay with you...I know you are keeping secrets. I know you have lied. I know there is more to this ship than what you say but come what may, I will stand by you, and die with you."

# TOXIC WASTE

It was three in the morning according to the ship's time log programmed on Earth's Gregorian Time. Frankie contacted Alaska through a secure channel they had created to keep in touch without the *Slicer*, now officially renamed *Ra*, knowing anything about it. "Green room."

Caldwell finished putting on his pants, his hair still wet from their showering together, and asked what the green room was. Frankie said, "You trusted me enough to tell me things I know you wouldn't have told anyone else. Now, it's my turn to bring you to a place that Alaska and I use to vent about this ship. The green room is where no frequency can obstruct our privacy."

She touched his chest, caressed his skin, and a fine layer of hair. She heard him say, "Rakes don't love...they make you theirs. You become a possession, and they cherish you as though you are a gift from above, from Him." He looked up, but then down in to her eyes. "That's why I don't know how to say it, I don't know if what I feel is what you are looking for in me to feel."

"Just say what it is Rakes say, and I'll be happy."

He touched her face, looked deep in her eyes, and with the softest voice she had ever heard from him, he said, "You're mine." She held his hand close to her face, and kissed his palm. Deep inside she knew he had ignited a flame she thought was lost forever. "Only mine, forever." He leaned his head forward, his lips touching her forehead. He kissed her as if he knew what they were about to face might put their lives at risk.

Now that Caldwell had put on his Captain's shirt, they both walked out of her quarters. Caldwell walked by her side, heading for the secondary elevator, that would bring them to the engineering floor at the back of the ship. At the elevator, Caldwell asked where they were heading. "Down below." The elevator had translucent walls, letting neon lights illuminate the half-moon shaped cylinder, as they were going lower in decks. The smell reminded Frankie of mechanic garages, her uncles owned one in her younger years. They went past the engineering and mechanics decks. Frankie could see Caldwell's facial expression changing, and he was always looking at the door. Caldwell's eyes opened wide, and Frankie wondered what he feared. Despite knowing that the lower they went, the more dangerous it could be if an attack were attempted on the ship.

The elevator stopped, and Frankie immobilized the door from opening. "We are at the toxic deposit and waste level. Everything here is what is unrecyclable. Way below, and away from engineering, of course. I must ask you, Jason, if you are an Android." Frankie saw Caldwell's brows lowering in the center as his head leaned forward staring at her. "To isolate ourselves from the rest of the ship, or whatever might listen outside of it, Alaska, and I created an ionic environment. Not enough to disrupt our mechanism, but it could hurt some, Android functions. So, Caldwell, are you an, Android?"

"No."

Frankie almost refused to believe him, but she had watched him bleed. However, she was told, androids were now confused as humans in the twenty-sixth century, so what did she know. They walked out of the elevator, and Caldwell kept close to Frankie, who guided him through the dark corridors. Lime green vapors came out of enclosed transparent shielding. Toxic waste left by the engine was filling the available tanks, and soon, would need to be discharged. Without the possibility of moving, sadly, *Ra* was stuck accumulating the waste. It was better inside than out, as it could, if they were unlucky, be used against them, which would vaporize the crew.

They walked through a dark corridor in low lighting. It was passageways, with large imposing rubber-like columns which were placed as support beams. Behind a large cargo like a bunker, Frankie saw Alaska accompanied by Wolf, Madsen, and Dr. Gillman. None of them had been aware of Alaska and Frankie's secret hideout. "How long have you girls been hiding here?" Caldwell asked, pointing at the two of them, "Ever since she came on board. We both decided it would be a healthy choice to have a place to vent about the ship, the crew, and…um, you, Sir." Caldwell pointed at himself, then looked at Frankie. "You did send me unarmed on missions." Yet, as she noticed his eyes squinting, Caldwell seemed confused.

Alaska scanned the environment with her ocular lenses, and backed up her analysis with the bracer scans. "Okay, it is safe for us to speak here. No one can hear us anywhere. The ionic shower is blocking all transmissions. All anyone might hear would be white noise. Let's get down to business."

Alaska first mentioned the danger *Ra* was in at the moment. Without its FTL engine working correctly, or as it was supposed to, she noticed that her system might have been damaging its original propulsion system. The backup system was functioning so far, but only to maintain all the other structures running, i.e. the life support, and artificial gravity engine. "I will be working on that Binary Core confinement after this meeting. I have chosen three of my most trusted crew to work with me, and they are sworn to secrecy. I do not want this structural device to fall into the wrong hands. If I suspect anything, Dr. Gillman has agreed to use her hypnosis, and erase the memory of the Core altogether."

Frankie watched Caldwell nod, his lips tightly sealed. With his arms crossed over his chest, he seemed quite uncomfortable in the environment although the odor might have been getting to him. It was a large deposit of toxic waste, oil, fat, blubber, human waste, and many other things, but she knew it was something else.

"Now that we know the Rakes are after this ship, and most likely Frankie—"

"They're not." Caldwell cut off Wolf without thinking twice, something he had never done. He would always let his crew finish their sentences before correcting them or adding to their statement.

"How do you know, Sir?" Wolf asked looking into the blue of his eyes, "Because I'm a Rake." Caldwell confessed.

Alaska, Wolf, and Madsen laughed until they noticed Frankie, and Dr. Gillman remaining silent. "The plot thickens," Alaska whispered. Frankie knew Alaska had fully trusted Captain Caldwell in the past, but not so recently, and now that revelation might have explained why. Nevertheless, Frankie reminded them that at this moment, he was their only hope out of the mess, and maybe, the key to repairing all the damage that had been done. "Or he's a spy," Madsen mentioned, but Frankie maintained that if paranoia found its way inside *Ra*, all would be lost. "He has led us this far. If he had been to report anything, he would've done it long ago, and we'd all be either dead, or part of the Dome."

All three agreed. It was now time for Captain Caldwell to reveal a few secrets about the Rakes. Also, what he knew about their intentions toward *Ra*, and Frankie. Maybe a few other well-kept pieces of information about the species, and their weaknesses. Caldwell did try to block his nose, the fumes were getting to him, but it wasn't the stank, it was more than that. Frankie recognized the signs: the sweat, the cracking voice, the eyes unable to focus, the constant movement of his hands, placing his shirt. She reached out to his hand. He tried to move it away, but she grabbed on. "Captain. No one hears anything here." "Sir, 2718 Caribbean rum?" Alaska asked, handing him her flask. He chuckled, smiled, and shook his head. Frankie knew what he wanted. He wouldn't take it out of pride, or scared one would tell on him, she didn't know.

"Wolf, where's that Irish whiskey I got you?" He took it out and shook the bottle before taking a mouthful. Handing it to Dr. Gillman, she squeezed one of her fangs into each flask giving it a harder kick for the two crewmates.

"So, you taught them that old trick, Gillman?" The Doctor shrugged, and smiled, "Sorry, we were not that special, Sir."

Frankie didn't drink. Her compulsive personality pushed her to always be in control of her environment, and inhibition prevented her from ever being attracted to any kind of booze. She held Caldwell's hand, who still seemed uncomfortable showing affection in front of his crew. "Sir, you think Frankie didn't tell me about the steamy sex you had in the cargo room?" Frankie closed her eyes. She didn't want to face Caldwell's stare. The good news was that he still held her hand, the bad news was that she could feel his anxiety rising. "She did, didn't she? Well, I hope it was all good." The crewmates smiled, "She seemed quite satisfied, and wanting more." No, Frankie wouldn't take a look.

A discharged of fumes was released, the vent opened to purify the breathable air, while the opening of the gas release was exposed behind the translucent walls. It created a loud noise. Caldwell jumped, and said, "I was General Zad-yreL back on Scorpio. Back then, we had only just started being called Rakes. Our species was known as Legion." He swallowed his saliva slowly, and cleared his throat, "Before I became a General, I was a physicist, and worked on many experiments, including a replica of a binary black hole system. I did research while in the military, alongside other scientists, to associate the decline of health in our space military with the engine. When it was proven, the government ordered us to destroy all of the evidence, and never mention it again. Many scientists revolted against their decision and disappeared. I, for my part, decided to eradicate the threat all-together when I was made aware of our government making a deal with the Dome to feed them the blueprints to the binary engine. I was no fool, the corruption of what a binary engine could do was evident. They wanted to own the Dome."

Frankie couldn't believe what Caldwell revealed next, "I took a spacecraft, i.e. *Ra*, loaded it with a dark matter bomb, and released it on Legion. I committed genocide. My own people." He kept going without remorse, "The ones that are alive now, are those who colonized our secondary planet. Some are those who were already in spacecrafts." Alaska asked how it was possible when so many Rakes were at large. "Legion was the home world, but we had a colonized dwarf planet. While it is true to say Legion are Rakes, not all Rakes are Legion."

Frankie gasped. Now she knew why some appeared larger, and taller, while others were slim, and capable of walking on ceilings. "So, some Legion made it to the Dome." Caldwell nodded. "They are attempting to reproduce the recipe, but it was so well-kept secret, that so far, they have failed. Zachariah keeps on coming back to *Ra* due to its unique engines. He knows the codex must hold something we're all missing to finish the puzzle. We're talking about a spaceship. What's the most basic function of a starship: travel between star system. Would it be so far-fetched to believe *Ra* might go farther than solar systems? What if *Ra* is what the Dome, the Alliance, and the Rakes want because it can either travel way faster than any other ship or because it goes where no other starship can? I believe it logical to draw this conclusion. Those, I believe, are their suspicions and so are mine. You, Frankie, might be seen as the missing link between the engine and the ship."

"You believe *Ra* is capable of going faster than a faster than light ship?" Wolf asked.

"I believe they believe it is."

All agreed that the ship had too much power for one race to rule over. The team now feared many races would come after it. The Dome wasn't a species, but a court of many allied together to conquer all that could be subjugated. *Ra* was the beginning of their quest, it was a prize that could permit them to enslave others faster than ever before. The Greys, wisely, got rid of their knowledge. They put it all in one vehicle, Frankie.

"Zachariah knows she knows, that they know, we now know." Wolf said, Alaska taking his flask away, added, "What's that Zachariah's intention? Frankie told me about the torture he practiced on you, and how close you seemed to have been at one point in your lives. It cannot be just a coincidence that he happens to appear when you are in charge of

*Ra* and beat him to the punch by taking Frankie with you. Is he with the Dome or against it? What's his deal?"

Caldwell shrugged, "I don't know." Frankie could tell he was telling the truth. He looked around, his eyes moving in empty space, "I don't know. All he said was that he had been in a relationship with Frankie for ten years and was aware that she had the Grey gene. He must've followed *Slicer* from the moment we were scanning for her DNA and saw how we kept going back to Alpha Earth over the Québec province."

The meeting was about to end, when Madsen asked, "So what's the plan now?" Caldwell said that first, they needed to make the Binary Core. Then meet with the source of all their problems, and destroy them. It wouldn't be an easy pill to swallow, but Caldwell refused to divulge all of his secrets in one meeting. It was enough, for now, to know he was Legion. He was on their side. His species was responsible for creating the Rakes, and were part of the Dome, maybe, "Part of the Dome, their plan was to take over it."

"For now, we need to get *Ra* back in shape, and get the fuck out of Rake space."

Caldwell was about to gently pull Frankie toward him, when she said she would be working on the Binary Core with Alaska. She was one of the three she trusted the most to handle the construction. He wanted to put a stop to her decision, but she reminded him, "I'm the only one with Grey knowledge. I will be able to fix the container, then they can receive the binary engine, and prepare the ship for the change in FTL."

Caldwell closed his eyes, unhappy with her decision but she was right. She kissed him, and said, "I'll be back for dinner." Caldwell was worried. For a moment it almost felt as if the whole world around them collapsed, and only the both of them were left alive. "The binary engine made many alien races sick. You saw what it did to King. It's like rabies, but you never die, you crave fresh, alive flesh. Next thing you know, your body is breaking into this insidious creature that we keep fighting." He had both hands on each side of her face, holding it dearly, "I can't, I can't let it happen to you, Frankie. You're...you're mine."

Frankie stepped away. She was his, and she knew it, but she said, "I'm the only one capable of making this happen besides you. Right now, *Ra* needs its Captain in his chair. This is why you came for me, remember? I carry the knowledge, and I will complete this mission."

# LET'S GET COOKING

Alaska, and Frankie were in the engineering laboratory with the two other trusted crewmates working on the shell to contain the Binary Core. The laboratory had silver grey walls, and long rectangular lighting was attached to the ceiling and projected the necessary light for each project. Many laboratory tables were placed parallel to one another. The cabinets on the wall were filled with chemistry sets and the different fluids necessary for experiments. The back wall served as a whiteboard when not being used as a computer monitor. The touch screen could be used in many ways, serving all scientists on board. Most recently, for the past four years, it had helped both Frankie and Alaska.

Alaṣka might have been the commanding engineer of *Ra*, but her first, and foremost career back in the twentieth-seventh century was astrophysicist. Alaska possessed two Ph.Ds., one in astrophysics, and one in theoretical physics, which specialized in quantum-loop gravity, and her hero was Neil deGrasse Tyson. Often Alaska would ask Frankie about him, because she still read his books, and remembered watching him on television, back when she lived on Alpha Earth in the twenty-first century.

Alaska had the math, written on white cardboard by Caldwell himself, on the table toward the back of the laboratory. Both were looking at his handwriting. The mathematical equation was one that should've set Frankie's brain on fire. Instead, she heard Alaska say with a ghostly voice, trembling, and hesitating, as her arms crossed over her chest.

"We're not talking about antimatter here, or gravitational waves...

we're talking about one of the most destructive forces in the universe, Frankie. If we succeed, one false move, and we might end up where all hell breaks loose."

Frankie was about to come clean about a part of her life she had never told anyone, except Caldwell. She had kept it to herself for so long that now they were about to create something that could disrupt the fabric of the galaxy. She said, "I'm a ufologist from CaldTech Industries, Alaska." Her friend stared at her. "I studied alien conspiracies, abductions, cover-ups, scientific implications, and everything in between." She remembered her life at CaldTech Industries for a brief moment. "I knew so much about the subject, that I was hired at CaldTech to work on top secret files. That's when my theory about the company being allied with aliens came true. I worked on differentiating alien artifacts, as we've been visited by more than one species. But to work at CaldTech, they needed bloodwork, and saw I was different." Frankie took a deep breath, looked into Alaska's eyes and revealed her long-held secret, "I went out with General Ash Zachariah for ten years."

Alaska's eyes rounded, but asked why she felt compelled to share her story at that moment, when all was critical in Rake space. "Because, I don't want any secrets between us, and if I die in this mission I want you to know the truth." Her eyes blurred, "I met Ash when I worked at CaldTech Industries. When I saw the memory of Jason being tortured by Ash, he even told him about our relationship. He said he protected me by telling the Dome and the Rakes that I wasn't the one they were looking for, but they caught up on his lie and that's how he ended up infected by the Rake's mutation." Alaska held Frankie's hands, "Ten years...so you guys were..."

"Intimate. Yes. He taught me martial arts, shooting, everything you see me do. It's almost like he knew what could happen to me and made sure I'd be able to defend myself."

"He loved you...and still does." Alaska said, while moving her head, "What else do you know that you're not telling me?"

"Ash is a biotechnologist. I believe he might know what happened to Nakamo. He knows how to save him. I'm sure of it."

Suddenly, a cool, swirling breeze took over the laboratory, invading the space. Green particles arose, "You two, take everything with you, and leave, now!" The two workers ran out of the lab following Alaska's orders, leaving her, and Frankie alone with the materializing alien in the middle of the room. Alaska quickly took the cardboard, and hid it in her bra below her tank top. Frankie knew who would materialize before her.

Everything came rushing back in her mind, memories of him training her into the killing machine she had become.

"Jake Carlson," she said when Zachariah appeared before her. She saw his brow arching, the human name he used had startled him. Frankie looked at his green cargo pants, holsters tied to his belt on both thighs, arm braces on each forearm holding screen monitors to display information on the ship, and himself. His light brown hair tied at the back of his head left his face uncovered. His one remaining lavender eye fixed on Frankie, who felt repulsed by the mere thought of what they had once shared.

"No...Frank, I...I never thought I'd see you again. I never wanted for us to end like this or at all. I am sorry for what I did the other night. I don't know what took over me."

"We shouldn't focus on the past, because it won't change, but on the task ahead. Why do you keep coming back here? And don't you dare say it's for me."

Zachariah raised his head. His eyes, even the one entirely scarred and blind, seemed to fix on Frankie, who swallowed her tears back, unwilling to succumb to the memory of a decade spent together as he walked forward. She showed no fear, despite knowing he could have appeared anywhere else, yet it was twice now that he beamed directly to where she stood. Somehow, he had a track that led to her.

"I never lied to you, Frankie. You knew who I was from the moment we met. I said I was part of an alien race called Legion. It is still true. CaldTech knew about me, they knew about you, and we were working together to keep you safe."

"Why?"

"Because I love...loved you. Because CaldTech knew you had to be kept a secret. I'm not like Caldwell, Frankie. I don't lie, and I don't hold secrets. I despise deceptions, and I would be damned if I let anything happen to you." He took a deep breath, "I left because I had to, not because I wanted to."

Frankie somehow knew he had left for a good reason and for over four years she wondered what happened to him and if he was safe. Despite standing in the light and remembering their love, laughs, memories, Frankie remained cold to his presence. She let him come forward, but tried to keep her distance. He reminded her of joyful moments, until she asked him with a firm voice, "Now, at this very moment, why are you here?" She used a tone that had no emotions, and she could almost hear his heart within his chest breaking, "Remember, you never lied to me."

Ash straightened up, and he suddenly looked more imposing than he had before. His voice lowered, and he addressed Frankie through his jaw piece, "Remember the picture on my desk? Remember the day I took it, and how happy we were? I thought about requesting asylum on Earth and marrying you." Frankie asked again the reason for his presence, "Please, don't make me lie to you." Frankie glanced at Alaska, "When I left Earth, I erased CaldTech Industries' files of you and deleted The Supra Project. The tablet I held before you the last time contains everything CaldTech collected about you."

Frankie gulped, that was the information that her old bosses used to keep about their employees. This information, however, concerned Frankie, and her past. An experiment that had been conducted on her, and all she could think about was how many times Zachariah might have been reading those files. "I can't read it, not because of my lack of trying. It is encoded with the same type of codex the Greys used for this ship, and that means CaldTech's founder might have been either like you, or working with Greys."

"What, are you going to give us the tablet out of the kindness of your heart?" Alaska asked, stepping in front of Frankie as if to show Zachariah would have to get through her to get to her friend.

With his hand held forward, Zachariah moved to hand Frankie the electronic tablet. But, she didn't move. So, he slid it across the table in her direction asking her to analyze it to confirm there was no virus, or no malicious intention. She lifted her eyes as he asked, "Remember the night I said there was nothing you could do that would make me hate you?" Frankie nodded, and feared that man died a long time ago, probably when he lost his eye trying to get something he shouldn't have had. "I still hold on to it. I still remember you, us. I swear if I could, I would go back, and we'd be together forever. I'm sorry I had to lie to you."

Frankie quickly lost the shy smile on her face because he had never lied to her. Alaska grabbed the electrical tablet and the moment Frankie looked up at him, her mouth slightly opened she frowned, "Why?" she whispered, hurt that he broke his own word that he had to lie. "Rakes will keep attacking, Frankie. Nothing will stop until you are in the hands of the Dome, us, or the Alliance. I can't stop them because I want you, Frankie." She closed her eyes. She felt her eyes filled with tears, but none dripped down her cheeks. Alaska was still working on the tablet, Frankie reached her side down her knee-high boots and retrieved a knife. Zachariah stepped away from the light, and opened his arms. "Nothing you could do to me would make me hate you, Frank. I believe we are meant to be together. Even our galaxy couldn't keep us apart."

That simple thought frightened her. She felt chills grabbing onto her

## A.D WAYNE

spine like goo, and crawling up to the back of her neck when she felt all her hair standing straight. She gulped, and watched Zachariah dematerialize before her eyes as a swirl of lime green orbs took him away. Alaska's voice stated, "We need to get the fuck out of here, now!" Alaska turned on all monitors, typing she said, "Caldwell's Binary Engine equation is now entered." She put in quotations, and then saw, "Access denied?" She turned to Frankie, and asked for her to enter her access code higher than her own, as she was first in Command. Frankie typed, "J011818." Then, "Access Denied." Something was wrong, and so Alaska added, "Frank, the equation is locked. If we don't have access to it, we can't alter or encode it, and someone who revoked our access can steal it."

"He lied to me." Frankie took the tablet off Alaska's hand and shook it in front of her eyes, "There is no virus or threats on this tablet, because this tablet is empty! He was bate."

The magnitude of what the equation implied was more than what anyone could conceive. Frankie ran out of the lab with Alaska following her, and they both quickly headed to the bridge. The Captain's chair held all access to the entire starship and critical systems. She paced on the bridge, the room was in a half-full moon shape, and held ten people working at all times, beside the Captain. Two pilots, including Helle Madsen's husband, Erik, at the front, one navigator behind their station on the right. There were two engineers who were keeping their eyes on the ship's status behind the Captain's chair, and one analytical technician on the far left, stood beside an exo-geomatics technician. There were also two officers continually listening to space debris, and transmissions, while the weapons specialist, Cadet Zwally, stood by in case of an attack.

"Commander?" Caldwell said as he suddenly stood up surprised to see Frankie barging onto his bridge with Alaska. "No time." Frankie accessed *Ra*'s computer directly from Caldwell's monitor screen on the side of his chair. She entered all of his accessing code, and granted rights, to manually bypass all ship's commands. "Someone locked you out, Sir." Alaska said, "Frank, the only one who could, is that fucking blonde bitch of an Admiral." Caldwell, lost, and confused, looked at Frankie for an explanation. She gave a quick glance at Alaska, who revealed what happened in the laboratory, including the sudden materialization of Zachariah.

*Frankie, why do you keep doing this to yourself!* She thought to herself, *why do you have to keep choosing aliens to have sex with!* It was now logical to think maybe Zachariah, and the Admiral were working together. He wanted her. She wanted Caldwell. Maybe, just maybe she was overthinking everything.

"Wait, all my accesses are denied?" Caldwell asked incredulously.

"Not if I can prevent it and hack the revoking access system."

The computer displayed codes Frankie had never seen before. But she intended to restore *Ra* the way she was supposed to be, which was a Grey ship. For that to happen, she had to reset the entire programming system of the ship, and shut down every single procedure including life support, and tactical. For eighty-two seconds, the ship would be defenseless, adrift in the most dangerous space possible to them at the moment. "Ready?" Frankie asked, looking for an order from her Captain, he lifted his hands, shrugged, and looked at the monitor screen displaying space outside the ship. "Have at it! I know nothing about that shit so, by all means. Give me back my ship."

The intercom turned on, and Captain Caldwell announced with his stentorian voice after Frankie nodded in his direction, "This is your Captain. Reset Mode is on. This is not a drill. Everyone has ten seconds to tie themselves to the ship using the magnet on the back of their uniform. Take two deep breaths, and release before holding all the air you can in your lungs for eighty-two seconds. The ship's magnet is activated in six, five, four—" Frankie looked up at everyone on the bridge who activated the magnetic function of their boots, now glued to the ship's floor. She waited for Caldwell's countdown, "Three, two, one." He nodded, and Frankie turned off the entire ship.

As if she had entered a code for safe mode, a black screen appeared with hieroglyphs in gold like an archaic computer. Frankie started typing faster than anyone could've followed her fingers. The weightless environment made it harder for her to focus on her task while the temperature kept dropping way quicker than she thought it would. Alaska stood by Frankie's side, holding the equation in her line of sight. She felt like her stomach moved into her throat, and she realized they probably were upside down already. Moving fast across Rake Space, with no shields or deflector to keep space debris away. Like a wreck underwater, Frankie heard the body of the ship decompressing. Still, twenty seconds to the countdown. Frankie had to enter the algorithm to be ready for the binary engine fuel to be collected. The codes entering the computer to command its every move, the new system was available to power up. She only had a few more lines to add before the ship would turn on again. "Done!"

The lights came on, releases from all vents were heard like a strong gale of wind. Everyone could finally take in a deep breath. They could be released from their emplacement where they were magnetized to hold still. Everyone was breathless, either sliding to the floor or with their heads near their knees when leaning forward, Frankie realized she could've kept going for another hour. The Grey gene made her quite resistant to a weightless environment. She was a bit nauseated, but nothing else seemed to have been a problem. The intercom on again, "This is your Captain. We are now back online. Everyone report to Dr. Gillman's office when called. In the meantime, keep working on maintaining the ship, such as it is. Caldwell out."

The intercom was an essential way of communicating with the entire ship. It had not been affected by the revoked access coding, that had been implemented earlier through the LSS system. Now, Caldwell looked at Frankie with his eyes wide, brows elevated, and tightly sealed lips. She nodded, "All systems are back to normal, except that it works according to the *Ra* system, and not LSS. Holoprojectors of its appearance are now down. Officially, this is now a ghost ship. It cannot be seen by the Alliance or the Rakes. Its serial number, just like its emitting transmissions, are encoded by Grey codes. Those are not readable to any other ship at the very least in this sector, if not all quadrants of the Milky Way. We are ghosts, Sir." Despite the sigh of relief from Caldwell, Frankie awaited the arrival of the Admiral, who like Alaska said, could've been the only one taking away the Captain's privilege of running the ship. She had made herself clear in the past. She wanted Caldwell at any cost, and despised Frankie. The next logical step was to spy on the Admiral as they needed to confirm the theory before she would barge on the bridge, yet nothing happened.

Frankie waited a few more minutes. Since nothing seemed about to happen, she looked over to Alaska who confirmed her thoughts. They needed a binary engine retainer. LSS ships belonging to Liberty were secretly apart from the Alliance, and worked on a different FTL. Therefore, the operating system in engineering was now entirely different than *Ra*. Whoever had camouflaged the entire ship, did a great job doing so. Frankie said, "Now, we need to board a Rake ship." The Captain categorically refused and ordered them to fix the existing retainer to fit the fuel. Alaska stepped in and reminded the Captain of his obligations to the safety of the crew. His duty to the entire spaceship that could soon fall into the hands of wrong people. It could do a lot of damage, not only to the quadrant, but the whole galaxy.

"We need binary fuel retainers, and we need them yesterday. Admiral Heikki won't stay silent long either. She's probably only waiting for the ship to be ready to receive you know what. The retainers need to be in place, working, and we both know binary fuel needs a special dispenser. The energy it retains cannot be released all at once. The mechanic we have now is not adequate for that shit despite technically being a Grey ship. It was modified to fit LSS and fool them, now, we need it all back to its original purpose."

"For fuck's sake!" Caldwell shouted as he kicked his chair, "This could've all been avoided if I had made sure none of

them survived."

"Blaming the past doesn't do much for the future, Captain." Frankie whispered before

Alaska reminded everyone, "Binary fuel won't collect itself."

Everyone on the bridge looked confused, moving toward the commanding chair, and squinting their eyes. A few asked what binary fuel was. "Binary, like a gender?" Others asked if they were drunk, and one asked, "Have you gone to the proper engineering school, because the opposite of dark matter is antimatter." Alaska faked a laugh, and ordered all of them back to their posts. When Caldwell finally nodded, he said they would go back to the same Rake ship they had infiltrated before. Remembering when Commander King was infected, he grabbed Frankie by the arm, and said, "Not you, not this time." Frankie released her arm, and said, "Without me, this mission will fail. I'm the only one who knows what we need to find, and how to use a white hole."

Gasps from all around, Caldwell raised his head, and looked at Frankie. There was no point in hiding what the equation really meant anymore, just like there was no need of calling it binary. "Isn't that it? *Ra* will be pulled to the white hole situated to the coordinates you gave Alaska, and me. Then, the ship will collect its residual energy, and use it as a propelling system for the Binary Engine. The fuel itself, is contained inside the Halo Sphere. To succeed, we need the Rakes' reverse system, because if all we know is correct, while a black hole pulls you in, a white hole pushes you out. We will need the reverse system to hold us in place when we'll arrive at the destination, just like we need the right magnet to pull us to it." Caldwell's head leaned forward, "The price is too high to pay." Frankie looked at the bridge officers, "What you have heard here will stay within these walls. If I hear you have spit out one word that has been said here, you'll be thrown in the brig with three holes in your skull. Have I made myself clear?" All answered, "Aye, Sir."

# GUNS AND ROSES WITH THORNS

Frankie asked, as officially as she could, for Caldwell to follow her to the armory. They walked following the white lighted corridor with silver metallic walls, garnished with many monitors showing different factions of the ship. Cameras above their heads were hung from a pipeline, following each possible corner, leaving no place to hide. Frankie walked past many other crewmates, either from maintenance, science, engineering, or security. Everyone was on high alert, especially since the ship had become an easy target, floating in Rake Space.

"You are going to allow me to have weapons this time."

"This time, what do you mean by that? You are the one who chose to go unarmed." Caldwell looked confused.

Frankie squinted her eyes and fixed on Caldwell. With an unpleasant voice, she reminded him of all the missions she was sent on without weapons. She recalled the times he said it might trigger her Grey gene, that the Captain stepped away from her. He held his hand up before his chest in a gesture of surrendering and replied, "I've always authorized you to have weapons. Never have I forbidden one of my crew to be unarmed, especially my main asset."

That was impossible. Frankie knew about Caldwell forbidding weapons. Even Commander King had gotten into a fight with the Cadet monitoring the Decoder room. "I've heard that. I didn't know why it was an issue, or how I was dragged into it for that matter." Frankie doubted King was to blame, since he had wanted her to be safe since they had met, and so had Frankie growled out the name. Heikki. The only one capable of benefiting from her death, would be "Admiral Heikki."

Frankie, and Caldwell kept walking toward the elevator, going two decks above the bridge where the armory was placed. They walked toward the back of the ship, and he asked her how many missions she had completed without weapons as he recalled never seeing her with anything else than knives or borrowed weaponry from the Rakes she had killed. "All of them." She glanced at Caldwell who tightened his lips. By that change on his face, she could tell he desired nothing more than to give hell to the Admiral. It warmed her heart to know he would, but it was not the time or place. "If it had not been for your martial art skills or Grey gene, you could've died!"

They approached the armory where a crewmate stood before the rows of weapons. Frankie made sure Caldwell understood. Until they knew more about the Admiral, she should be left alone, so as not to trigger anything suspicious. Frankie believed it would force her to act prematurely on those beliefs. Before the counter, Frankie lifted her head, and turned the monitor toward her. She engaged the linking system from her ocular implant to the computer, and shared a weapon file with it, in order to reproduce her favorite weapon of all time. "The Beretta 93R is a fire handgun used by the military constructed toward the end of the twenty-first century on Earth." Frankie added her modifications to it based on a science-fiction movie character she quite admired. "Add to the Beretta 93R an elongated barrel with a husky compensator hidden in the shape of a casket. It will require a taller rear sight, because of the front. I want it capable of at least three-round burst mode. Make it capable of holding at least a fifty-round magazine. The color has to be black." After the modifications were given, she added, "Thank you, *Ra*."

The monitor displayed a blueprint of the modifications Frankie had added to the Beretta pistol, and she agreed to the specs, while seeing the white outline on a stone-grey background, with a 3D view of what the handgun and bullets would look like. It showed her how to load it safely and handle it. Despite being from Canada where weapons were outlawed, unless going through a rigorous procedure and training, Frankie knew how to handle a gun. Back in North America, she had been taught how to shoot a variety of weapons and had an eye for the target because of Zachariah. She approved the weapon and asked for two modified Berettas. The crewmate behind the counter said that Frankie wasn't authorized to wear defenses, and Captain Caldwell leaned over the counter, and asked who gave the order.

"You, Sir."

"Me?"

"Yes, you come here before every mission to make sure everyone understood that you didn't want Commander Stein wearing weaponry."

"How can I be on the bridge, and here at the same time, Cadet?"

"I don't know, Sir, but you were here a moment ago."

The man was sweating, and his eyes were covered in tears as his hands trembled. Frankie had never witnessed the fury of Captain Caldwell, but she suspected that it might have been quite immobilizing for the crew. He approved the handguns, and the crewmate bowed saying it would take about ten minutes for the 3D Weapon Printer to forge the arsenals. Caldwell slid his large imposing hand over his face, and mentioned that someone had to have used something to camouflage their appearance. Frankie knew he referred to himself, having tricked an entire part of the galaxy into believing he was human. Naturally, other species might have shared a morphing capability somehow, and they had either kept it a secret or had ways to change their appearances.

"Maybe, they have telepathic abilities, therefore they are capable of presenting a false appearance. What do we truly know about the Nordic species?"

"Not much. Nordics are quiet about themselves, and other than believing that they are the best there is in the entire galaxy, not much is known."

"Are you saying that this Alliance thing didn't require a full dissection of every single aspect of their planetary situation, and species?"

"That's utopian thinking."

"No shit...on the other hand, it got me this far."

"What?"

Frankie had a plan on a galaxy level. However, first, she needed to take care of some Rakes, and she would be deadly. Now that she knew Captain Caldwell was not behind her not wearing any weaponry while on mission, she felt more confident in her feelings toward him. She felt his hand softly holding her in place. His hands were gripping her left upper arm and pulling her near him. He leaned in to whisper so no one would hear him. Caldwell spoke to her in a manner that no Captain should do to his first in command.

"Why did you agree to make love with me again and again, if I was willing to have you go unarmed to a spaceship full of flesh-eating monsters?"

She looked up into the sapphire blue of his eyes, "Because I wanted you to be mine."

His eyes closed, "Don't ever do that again. Don't let your feelings blind your eyes, Frankie. Your life might be more precious to me than everything in the galaxy, but it should be worth even more to you." He held her face in his hands,

"Promise me, that you won't let what I mean to you cloud your judgment."

"Wouldn't you?"

He sighed, "I've done it a thousand times already, and I would do it a million times more."

The crewman came back with the weapons, and ammunition. Frankie took the two Berettas, and even though she wasn't expecting the weight to be that heavy, she hid her surprise well. She asked for the double holster to attach to her belt, and thighs. Then, she said, "I want to kukri knives." Five minutes later when the Cadet laughed as he handed Frankie the knives, he said, "Can we go more primeval than that?" Frankie quickly grabbed the man by the collar and pulled him toward her. "Now that you have the blade right below your jaw with pressure against your flesh, and I make you feel like a meat bag, tell me, how does it feel?" The man looked toward Caldwell who shrugged, "Well, Cadet?" The crewman gulped, sweating he answered as he looked into Frankie's hazel eyes, "Scary, Sir." She let go. "If I'm going to get what we need to save your ass, and the others' on this ship, I'll do it on my terms. Besides, I've never seen anyone capable of dodging a bullet. The kukris are for a personal purpose."

Frankie stepped into the locker room. She put on her khaki cargo pants, and a grey sport-cut tank top under a black fitted one. She attached the holster to her belt and thighs, and put on her boots. Later, Frankie twisted her black hair on the top of her head into a bun, and held it in place with a lime green scrunchie. She secured the two modified Berettas she now called, the Murphys. She walked out, and walking by Caldwell's side, they stepped into the Decoder room across the corridor where Wolf, Madsen, and Alaska waited for them to arrive, armed and ready to be transported to the Rake ship.

The room was dark, as always. The security guard overlooking the monitor, and the crewman in charge of the Decoder were looking at the screen, evaluating the status of the Rake ship. Frankie was about to join her crewmates when Caldwell stopped her. He looked at the guard and officer, and said, "Dismissed." The air was cool, and the tension was thick. Frankie asked what was wrong, and she saw him pull a chain from his pocket with a double pendant. One was shaped like an oval, and she read, "Male. General Zad-yreL. Scorpio. Legion. 156DD89B-XY." The other pendant was a cross. "Is this...?" Caldwell nodded, "It's the dog tag that I have left because I threw the other in the dirt before I left Scorpio. I got the cross from the first human I had met who said, 'Godspeed' to me. I asked what it meant, and he gave me a Bible, with that cross in it. Because I've always wanted to be human, I attached it to that chain. Now, I want it to be yours, so you will always have a piece of me with you...you're never alone. I'll be in your blood, close to your heart when you face the unknown." Frankie wished she had something to give in return. Caldwell leaned in, his lips pressed against her own, and he held her face close to his own as he whispered, "You've given me a reason to fight. Just promise me you won't let me put your life in danger." Frankie looked up into his eyes, "You're mine." She whispered, "I love you."

Frankie stood between Alaska, Madsen, and Wolf. All four were holding their weapons ready to fire. A shower of starlight swirled around them, and soon they vanished, bringing the quartet onto a ship that they knew was still full of flesh-eating monsters.

# NAKED LIGHT

2200 Hours, 19th of October 2510
(Gregorian calendar,)
Milky Way Galaxy, Rake Space, Scorpio Debris
Rake ship — UUS Cerberus II, Decoder Room.
Mission: Recovery.
Ship status: Sustainable.
Rakes: 132 — 80 in stasis, 52 dead, 13 alive.

"I guess our adjustments are working now. Stasis doesn't equal dead." Madsen said as the quartet noticed the entire floor was emptied of Rakes. They lowered their weapons, but kept them tight in their hands. Frankie was leading the mission and she walked first toward the entrance, following the metallic wall, and glanced outside. No one. She listened to the ship as she closed her eyes, and saw almost as if she could x-ray the ship through her mind. She knew exactly where the aliens were, and suddenly looked for Zachariah, who she suspected had orchestrated a trap, but Frankie outsmarted him—or at least she hoped. She had the Grey gene at full capacity, and, "There's a prisoner."

Alaska walked over to Frankie, and said, "We're not here on a rescue mission, Frank. We're here to steal equipment, and maybe blow up this shit hole in the process!" Frankie disagreed with her best friend for the first time; and replied, "So now we're pirates and that is it, Commander?" Wolf took Alaska's side. The humidity of the ship fell onto their shoulders, and the smell of rotten flesh crawled up into their noses to settle in their lungs, leaving them filled with frustration. Frankie, supported by Madsen, said "This isn't up for debate. If you saw firsthand what the Rakes do to people like you and me, you wouldn't be so quick to reject the idea of saving another being. You'd feel the obligation, and weight of that being's life on your shoulders." She looked at Wolf, "I know for a fact that Dr. Gillman erased your mind, repeatedly, because you weren't able to sleep at night. You don't remember, but I do. You walked into my room, and asked to sleep beside me because you couldn't stop crying in horror every time you closed your eyes. You'd see those pieces of shit biting down on your boyfriend's body. You tried to save him, and so, you shot him between the eyes."

Wolf's eyes squinted as he looked down. It sounded familiar, but he refused to remember. Frankie felt horrible retelling the story of the loss of someone so dear to her friend, but she felt as if she had no choice. "We need to save him, and whoever else has fallen victim to the Rakes. I won't leave anyone behind." Alaska finally agreed, and so did Wolf. Madsen nodded, and said, "let's go." The quartet followed Frankie. They were incapable of walking alongside the walls due to the spears planted in the grid floor, and so they relied on the darkness of the ship. The lighting was so low that they had to follow one another carefully. The prisoner was on the deck below, and when they found a vent large enough for them to squeeze through on the floor, Frankie used one of her kukri knives, and unscrewed the grid. They let themselves into the vent quietly, and started crawling, following Frankie's direction as she used her holographic projector to guide her on the best route to get into the cell where the abductee was being held captive. Madsen was the last to follow, on her back she used her heels to make her follow the trio her plasma gun pointed at anything that would dare show in her sight. Sniper eyed, she was one of the greatest assets on *Ra*.

The journey came to an end when they arrived on top of the brig. The grid screwed from the outside, so Frankie asked Madsen to use her plasma gun to cut through the grid. As the piece of metal was about to fall, Frankie caught it, and placed it to the side, so as not to make a sound. Alaska was about to step out, but Frankie stopped her. "You go to engineering with Wolf, you're the engineer the ship needs, and if someone comes I want you both to save yourselves. Take all you can and leave for *Ra*. Madsen will cover me while I rescue that male." Alaska nodded, "Aye, Sir." Alaska held Frankie's hand tight, both their eyes covered with tears, and it was as if they felt something would go terribly wrong. "Go!"

Madsen stepped out with her plasma gun pointed toward the door. She moved along the wall, and checked out each corner of the dungeon, before she signaled Frankie to come out. The humanoid male had both his hands chained above his head. He was bare chested which allowed Frankie to notice his muscular appearance. She grabbed the dog tag around his neck. It was in the Alliance shape, and she whispered, "Male. Lt. Cmdr. Michaël Leroy. LSS3172." She looked at the chains, and saw the large handcuffs holding a length of his forearms. His head leaned forward, he was unresponsive to her voice. But all the wounds on him seemed strange to Frankie who could now see in a full colored spectrum. "Something's off." She smelled the room. It had a different smell than burned flesh. She looked at the man's body, and though the bright red epiderma should've been enough to give his organic flesh away, something didn't add into the equation. Frankie grabbed the man by the chin, and lifted his head, she used her other hand to open his eyes. There was a rotating mechanism, like clockwork constantly adjusting by zooming in, and out.

"You're an Android."

Coming up behind her, Frankie heard Madsen whispering, "You know if Wolf were here he'd say something like 'we came all the way here for a fucking pile of computed files?' Me, I'm intrigued to know why he's been kept on an anthropophagi ship. Correct me if I'm wrong, but Rakes are not a bunch of Billy goats." Frankie agreed and listened to her advice.

Madsen reminded Frankie of the Grey gene, and how it had guided her well up until now. Frankie knew from her newly unlocked memories that the Greys were responsible for the androids being the saviors of Liberty. Madsen brought up, "Liberty is a planet that was once colonized by Earth's 'rejects.' The Androids were active in the war and took the humans of Liberty's side. Now, they're family." Madsen knew about their history quite well. Frankie looked at her bright red braided mohawk and feline eyes with her vertical pupils widening due to the faint lighting. "You know, Caldwell even saved Dryden from Earth and the Rakes once." Madsen added, "Androids were like the Grey's children, maybe the information on how to reanimate him is inside of you, Commander." Frankie had to focus on what the gene gave her. Maybe one detail would let her know exactly how to turn Commander Leroy on, and tell them why he was kept in the dungeon of the ship.

Another memory surfaced...

> 0400 Hours, 12th of May 2508
> (Gregorian calendar,)
> Milky Way Galaxy, Rake Space, Scorpio Debris
> *Slicer*, Medical Facility.
> Mission: Recovery.
> Ship status: Good.
> Crew: 234 — 2 in stasis, 21 dead, 203 alive.

FRANKIE WAS AWAKE, sitting on the medical bed, the pillows right against the wall. Above was a monitor adapted to her physiology, more specifically to her particular gene. She remembered the mission, and with Commander King by her side on the other bed, half sitting he turned his head over, and smiled through his finely trimmed beard. They had defeated the Rakes that time, coming after the *Slicer* following their intrusion on the ship to collect artifacts from the Greys. Frankie smiled back, but nothing was right, something was wrong she felt it. The tingling sensation in the back of her throat formed a burning ball while in her stomach the knot tightened. Suddenly, she hugged herself as she tightened her lips trying to fight the dark, and black embrace of fogging possibilities that would never happen, yet, kept taking over her brain. Frankie couldn't focus, and she wondered why, as it happened quite abruptly without any warning. Frankie looked to her right where she heard quiet footsteps and saw Dr. Gillman. She was holding a device that Frankie had brought back from the Rakes' ship. She mentioned suspecting it was to be used as a brain healing device. Instead it had been reprogrammed for torture by the Rakes.

The device looked like a fine chainmail gold glove going up to the elbow. While the one wearing the device would hover around the head of the patient, it would scan the brain, and leave a perfect three-dimensional holographic image of the patient's brain, and say what state of health the brain is in, either physically or psychologically, and provided a way to repair the damage done. Repairing seemed to require contact with the glove on the patient's head. Frankie didn't understand how the glove provided a cure, but she theorized that it needed a Grey to make it work for that purpose. Reprogramming it as a torture device had been achieved by a Rake engineer King took down.

As if a hammer had hit Frankie's skull, she fell forward. She felt King's embrace when he wrapped his arms around her to lift her up and hold her tightly against him. Holding her head, she rocked back, and forth, and tried not to scream. Her voice was cracking as she mumbled words she didn't understand the meaning of, "Nothing begins. Nothing ends." King kept asking her what she meant. She could hear his voice clearly, but wasn't able to say anything else, other than the words coming out of her mouth. Anxiety had completely overtaken her body.

"Dr. Gillman!" King shouted at the top of his lungs, "Frank needs help!"

"I do not know how to use this, but her brain scan shows something in her head."

"Do something! Use that Reptilian telepathic link of yours!"

"It doesn't work on Frankie. Her mental strength is too strong!"

"Even now?"

She heard their discussion, but their whispers still sounded like gibberish. She listened to the device being swung around. The sound of the gold chainmail clinking in the background as she held her head with her hands on each side of her temples. Tears were rolling down her face, as she then heard the automatic doors of the medical facility opening. She heard someone say, "Captain." Frankie listened to his walk, confident, as he paced to her bed. He asked what was going on and Dr. Gillman revealed her brain scans showing an anomaly. Something was blocking her from receiving further treatments. Their voices sounded more like background noises, and she felt King's hands moving up, and down her arms.

"From the ocular implants, we saw she clearly took a hit to the head by one of the Rakes. He was holding a baseball bat covered in nails. She was lucky to have dodged most of the hit, but there still was an impact."

"She seemed fine, she kept going, and got the glove, and the information—"

"With all due respect. Frankie was running on adrenaline, and probably her Grey gene. Now she's delusional."

"Can you do anything?"

"I can try, but I'm not sure it'll work."

Their voices were low, almost like whispers. By the tone, Frankie could recognize worry, and fear. The doctor, and the Captain cared for her, just like King did. But she was a puzzle, due to her twenty-first-century physiology. She was also a mystery due to her Grey gene that was slowly beginning to awaken within her blood. Frankie felt Dr. Gillman's hand below her chin, lifting her head to look into her Reptilian eyes. They were big and almond in shape. Her eyes had an overly full golden iris, and upright almond-shaped pupils. She could see a third lid blinking from the corner of her eyes to the other. Frankie felt as if she calmed down after feeling a sting on her arm.

"Everything will be alright, sweetheart. I won't hurt you, Frank, you know me."

Her voice was low and soft, holding compassion within it. Frankie always ended up trusting Dr. Gillman. Her voice, with the kind expression on her face was reassuring. Maybe it was misplaced of her, but Frankie loved reptiles. Every time she hung around Dr. Gillman, it reminded her of those old Earth animals she enjoyed so much. She never told anyone because she feared being disrespectful to Dr. Gillman, and Frankie had the highest respect for her. Despite feeling protected, and comfortable in her presence due to her appearance, she never said a word.

"I don't feel offended, sweetheart. I'm happy you think of lizards, and crocodiles in my presence. You can say that Reptilians are the amphibian version of humans. While your species walked out of the water, we stayed in. So, I do not feel insulted at all, I do see the resemblance myself."

"You heard that?" Frankie mumbled.

"Yes, right now I'm establishing a link between us, so I can see what's preventing me from helping you. I suspect your Grey gene has activated something else that was kept suppressed."

Frankie, although relieved, never thought Dr. Gillman could go into her mind, even though she knew about the telepathic abilities. What she knew stopped at the Reptilians developing links due to their physiology that permitted them to live underwater. They could be below for hours at a time; therefore, they needed a way of communicating. It had to be in a way other than a vocal language. Frankie felt nothing, no presence at all, it was like she was alone in her thoughts when Dr. Gillman revealed it was quite hard to keep a link. Then it disappeared completely.

"The link was interrupted. The best way I could describe it is static. That is Grey technology for sure. I know of no life form capable of this intensity. Also, at the stage Frankie is at telepathically, it shouldn't be present at all."

"Can't you try again?" Caldwell asked, while King insisted, "You can't quit!"

"There's nothing I can do telepathically! It's a barrier the Greys implanted to protect her suppressed knowledge."

A flash of white light took over Frankie's mind and had her grab the glove. She put it on. With great force, Frankie gripped Caldwell's forearm and activated his arm bracer device. It was ready to display any part of the ship like a holographic projector. She turned the monitor toward her, and scanned herself. Then, she covered her face with the glove. It attached to her skin like a magnet.

A pitch-black light aimed at Frankie and X-rayed her over again. She closed her eyes and felt as though trillions of microscopic ants walked over her skin, and went through her flesh. The light stopped, the glove disengaged from her skin, and the feeling of the jackhammer drilling through her skull stopped immediately. So, did the urge to continue to repeat the gibberish phrase.

"Tutankhamun."

"Excuse me?" Caldwell asked with a raised eyebrow as Frankie let go of his arm, and looked into the deep frost of his eyes. "Tutankhamun, what's that?"

"He was a young Egyptian Pharaoh, part of the eighteenth dynasty in ancient history, on Earth. Archeologists referred to his time period as the New Empire. Many referred to him as King Tut. He reigned between 1332 to 1323 BC. He died very young."

Dr. Gillman, Commander King, and Captain Caldwell all looked at her. They were probably thinking she was still wounded, and most likely suffering a severe concussion, which was true. The glove repaired it all, and through the process, she was given a piece of information that she thought might be of importance or may even be crucial down the road of her discovery of the Grey's codex.

"Captain, when I was hit on the head I was holding the device." Frankie pointed at the glove. "The reason Dr. Gillman wasn't able to get a stable link is because of a subliminal message that was implanted by the Greys to protect the knowledge they placed within me. It's the other appellation of Tutankhamun, the one directly linked to Aten."

"It makes...um...sense, I suppose?"

"I don't know why they chose him, I mean, the other way to spell his name means Living Image of Aten, which meant he looked like the sun.

Aten was the word ancient Egyptians used to refer to the sun's circle or disk shape."

"Maybe the sun in your solar system was special to them?" Dr. Gillman guessed.

"I think it was their point of reference, a way for them to always find my species, to find Earth."

Caldwell tried to understand Frankie's theory, but at the moment all she knew was that the appellation, Tutankhaten seemed to be a subliminal word for her to "power down" or entirely close herself to the outside world. It was a defense mechanism created by the Greys to protect what she carried.

"So, if I'm ever in danger, Captain, please use this to shut me down."

"You're asking me to hold your life in my hands, if I ever judge that you're putting yourself in danger, or fall into the enemies' hands?"

"Yes. I wish to keep what I have intact, so promise me."

"I promise...but only until your Grey gene fully awakens, and then you don't need it anymore. Then, I want that word gone of your head."

02200 Hours, 19th of October 2510
(Gregorian calendar,)
Milky Way Galaxy, Rake Space, Scorpio Debris
Rake ship — Cerberus II, Brig.
Mission: Recovery.
Ship status: Sustainable.
Rakes: 132 — 80 in stasis, 52 dead, 13 alive.

"They do have an obsession with the sun." Frankie held the Android's head, and said with a confident voice, "Tutankhaten." She also remembered, "*I guess it's a good thing Jason made sure it wouldn't be a subliminal message for me any longer.*" She heard a cough, and the Android was waking up. She knew the Androids were created by the Greys, and were built to deceive humans into believing they were part of their kind. They could also fake human reactions, such as gasping for air

or breathing.

"Are you all right?"

"Yes, I believe so...who are you?"

"I'm Commander Stein, and this is Lieutenant Madsen. Commander Leclerc is in the vent along with Lieutenant Wolf heading for engineering, where we'll meet with them after I free you from these handcuffs. Do you require assistance, or will you be okay on your own?"

"I'm in safe conditions for the moment. My programming is self-repairing as we speak."

"Let's get out of here while we can."

Frankie asked Madsen to change places with her. The plasma gun would be more useful in undoing the handcuffs mechanism. Frankie guarded the doors to the entrance of the dungeon. She could hear the metal melting. It was a good thing Madsen had keen vision, because her height was around five feet and four inches, and the Android stood about six and a hair. It had her on the tip of her toes, and quite a distance from the manacles. She succeeded in freeing Leroy and showed him to the vent. Frankie stopped him and asked why he had been taken prisoner by the Rakes, and why they had kept him alive when all they've ever run after was fresh organic meat.

"I was a part of Unit 8. I was one that I guess Dryden thought dead, since we are armed with a suicide chip. It was deactivated before I could set it off. Then, I felt something grabbing me, and I disappeared just as I saw the Khe soldier arriving to capture my unit."

Madsen held him in place, and asked, "Leroy, what was Unit 8?"

"Unit 8 had a mission to save all the OWLS Parliaments on Earth, and bring them back to Liberty. The secret part of our mission, though, was to find the rat among them that kept feeding the Dome information about Liberty's military defense."

Unit 8, Colonel Dryden, Khe soldiers, OWLS, Liberty. Frankie tried to make sense of what he was talking about. Madsen remembered briefings they once had about the subject of Alpha Earth.

"We're all from different timelines. Some of us are from way ahead in the future, while others like Commander Stein, are as far back as the twenty-first century." While they kept talking, Frankie remembered looking through files of time periods ahead of her own. She recognized the record holding Colonel Dryden's mission where he was saved by Captain Caldwell.

"Dryden was saved by Caldwell, it then sent Caldwell on his mission to save me from the Dome. Liberty knows about *Ra*. Madsen!" The sniper looked at her, "We must return to our ship. Correct me if I'm wrong, but we're their best officers and we're all away."

"Shit. That human Rake planed it!"

"Madsen, this Rake ship is a Trojan Horse."

Madsen asked what a Trojan Horse was, and the moment Frankie was about to tell them to move, Leroy explained the metaphor. Strangely enough, the Android had Earth history right. That proved that he had been captive long before the space-time continuum had been disrupted, and history rewritten. It also implied that he was from Frankie's timeline. They both looked into each other's eyes, and Frankie asked, "Those Khe soldiers, are they following Zachariah as well?" The, Android nodded, and said, "The Rakes are allied with the Dome, and they are coming for you."

"Khe soldiers?" Madsen asked, "The zombified OWLS working for the Dome?"

Leroy nodded, and added, "Khe soldiers are the Dome's army. Some are from Earths that experienced the Intergalactic War-1, they are those who defended the Androids and Cyborgs, aka, the Grey's children." He looked at Frankie, "Aka, an army of disposable people, unresponsive to anything, not even pain. Imagine now what they could do with Caldwell's ship, and its most precious asset."

"No offense, but why not create an army of...ahem...you?" Both hands on her hips, Madsen seemed to hope Leroy wouldn't feel offended by her question, as Frankie listened, but she already knew the answer. "The Dome lacked the technology. Even dissecting us wouldn't do them any good as we are armed with receptors, and we would simply turn to liquid metal. The Greys are our 'star parents.' There are only a fixed number of Androids that were made. The knowledge for creating us was given to only two people back on Liberty."

"Which proves that the Alliance is corrupt. The Supra Project also known as Division 8, Liberty was threatened by the Alliance."

The Dome knew about the Greys, the advanced technology, but only to a point. The 'Pandora's Box' was just out of reach. Frankie paced around, while Leroy and Madsen continued speaking of Khe soldiers in the background, and their recovery, through a false trafficking sanctuary. "Khe...I know the word, I've read it before...Khe" Frankie kept walking, faster, and faster she dug deeper into her memory when studying ancient history, and watching a documentary about old aliens visiting Earth. Suddenly, she stopped, and stared into the emptiness before her, and with a ghostly voice she said, "Khepri, Scarab...we're fucked!"

Frankie turned her attention back on Leroy and stared at him. With his head leaning forward, and his eyes going from right to left in an erratic rhythm he then straightened his head, with his eyes opened wide, he said, "Left or right we're fucked." Madsen, kept in the dark, asked, "Can someone tell me why we're this fucked?" She then kicked Leroy's shin with her black military boot, and said, "You, what's your deal, why did the Rakes keep you here for five years? It's not like you'd gain taste with time!"

The Rakes were known to devour their victims, and since he was no meat, she saw no reason for his stay. The Android appeared damaged, resisting with all he had within him to succumb to his own thoughts. Both Frankie, and Madsen could feel his pain because they had both felt it and had lived through it. The air in the dungeon seemed thicker, the light darker, and he said, "All, Androids are kept. We carry Grey history within ourselves. along with Earth history. However, only one has Earth Alpha's true history, and that's me."

Frankie concurred, and said, "Madsen, we need to go. This was a setup. We need to get back to *Ra* ASAP." Frankie ordered them all back in the vent, to follow directions to the engineer level. Madsen said, "Leroy first, Frankie, and I guard the back. If what you're saying is true Sir, you need to be protected. If he does carry enough information to put the entire universe at risk, you better follow his ass, and deactivate him if we're caught." Frankie nodded, "Right."

# MEANTIME END TIMES

2200 Hours, 19th of October 2510
(Gregorian calendar,)
Milky Way Galaxy, Rake Space, Scorpio Debris
*Slicer* Decoy — *Ra*, Main Bridge.
Mission: Guard.
Ship status: Sustainable.
Crew: 253 — 2 in stasis, 80 dead, 173 alive.

"Sir, Commander Leclerc and Lieutenant Wolf are in the engineering room. Their life signs are clear." Despite their ocular implant being turned on, dividing the main screen into four widescreens, allowing for Captain Caldwell to keep an eye on his most trusted crew members, he felt powerless. "Zwally, do we have the experimental beam ready?" Caldwell asked turning his head to his right to look over his shoulder at the tactical station, "Yes, Sir."

Standing up, unable to sit in his chair, Caldwell redirected his command to his ocular implant. He needed to keep an eye on the status of the ship. He heard his tactical officer, "Sir, Commander Stein found an Android from Unit 8." The Captain ordered Cadet Zwally to enlarge Stein's vision on screen. It was one of the units he saved back on his first mission for Liberty. Then, he saw his dark ginger hair, his pale skin with freckles. He recognized him, "Lt. Cmdr. Michaël Leroy. ALL3172." He heard his tactical officer affirming, "Yes, that is him all right." The computer's facial recognition confirmed the Android's identity. "Wait,

Sir. Commander Leroy is reported dead." Caldwell thought so too, then he whispered, "PBU."

The conversation was muted, the ocular implant limiting the interactions to visual. Caldwell refused to have no control over the situation, and heard his officer ask if Leroy was a threat to their mission. "Not yet. In the meantime, see if you can remotely turn on his suicide chip. We might have to use it, if he knows too much." He heard his bridge, "Aye, Sir!" Caldwell had followed every move, his focus now solely on Leroy. He wanted to understand why the Rakes had kept him alive for so long.

"I need answers! Why would a ship of flesh-eating fuckers keep a machine turned on? It can't be because they needed their bread toasted! Come on, help me out."

"The file says Leroy is from Alpha Earth, same as Commander Stein. If General Zachariah knows, he might have wanted to extrapolate all of Leroy's knowledge of Earth, and use it to lure Commander Stein into trusting him."

Caldwell turned to the screen, and walked toward it, "You motherfucking piece of circuit breakers. You gave out your knowledge for your life." Caldwell refused to sit and do nothing, but the suicide chip seemed to be out of reach for him. He could not order the destruction of the Android. "They are more complicated to hack than I thought, Sir." The Captain was losing his patience, and he feared for Frankie with every second that went by. "It's a setup. All of this is a setup." He backed away from the monitor. Caldwell knew the Android had been used for information. Frankie working for CaldTech Industries, meeting Zachariah, the *Cerberus II* is a decoy, *Fuck! Why didn't I see this coming*, he thought to himself.

His head down, he leaned forward as if he understood that he and his crew were set up for defeat. With his eyes closed, he quoted a man Frankie had spoken about throughout her years on *Ra*, teaching him about humanity. "War, in its fairest form, implies a perpetual violation of humanity, and justice."

"Sir?"

"Revenge is profitable, gratitude is expensive." Caldwell opened his eyes, and straightened up. He looked at his tactical officer, Cadet Zwally, and said, "Edward Gibbon, an eighteenth-century Englishman who wrote 'The Decline, and Fall of the Roman Empire.'"

His bridge crew stared at him, waiting for his command. Caldwell turned to the screen and looked at the Android through Frankie's eyes. He saw Lieutenant Madsen by the Android's side, talking, and about to enter the vent. He knew they'd be going toward engineering to join

Wolf, and Leclerc. Caldwell put his hand on the shoulders of his most trusted pilot, Erik Madsen.

"This is your Captain speaking!" Caldwell announced to the entire the ship after opening the channel, "Everyone, Hera Alert. This isn't a drill." All crewmen were ordered to protect *Ra*, and its most valuable assets at all costs. In this case, they were named, Frankie, Leclerc, Wolf, and Madsen. "Until further notice, I want everyone ready to attack the Rakes' warships or any other Alliance starship showing up." Caldwell then looked over his shoulder, and told Cadet Zwally, his new tactical officer, with a grave face, "Lock us out of the Alliance's channels." She looked around the screen, and lifted her eyes up to meet the Captain's gaze, who wondered why she looked so puzzled. "Commander Stein already did, Sir...we're on the OWLS' channels." He smiled, *"You're the smartest woman I've ever met, and you're mine."* His smile vanished when he snapped out of his daydream, and he glared at Zwally. He knew he could trust her, "If Admiral Heikki walks onto the bridge, I want you to order security to hold her to her quarters. Right now, we cannot trust anyone, understood?" She nodded,

"Aye, Sir."

Caldwell opened a private channel, and said, "Gillman, Watson, to the war room." Both responded with an affirmative and met the Captain in the silent quarters. The holographic table in the middle, showed Frankie's point of view throughout the ventilation tubes. All three stared in silence in the instant images received from the Rakes' ship. "I want to know what is to be expected from the Rakes, the Alliance, and the Dome." Caldwell's words were grave, and with his arms spread apart on the table, he leaned over to stare at Frankie's view. He added, "I don't know if you noticed, but right now, we're big, juicy, wounded prey, and most probably surrounded by a pack of hungry wolves." Caldwell didn't hide his thoughts, and he knew that all enemies were now surrounding *Ra*, waiting for Frankie, and Leclerc to make the engine work, while Madsen, and Wolf would retrieve the Android holding Alpha Earth's history. "One will get Frankie while the other will hold Leroy. The Alliance, and the Dome will get the history of Alpha Earth and have the ability to go back in time at the exact moment the Greys infiltrated Earth for the first time. They will steal their technology, and rewrite history. Their agreement might be short-lived at this moment, but it is quite effective nonetheless. The Dome and the Alliance somehow united for this specific moment. Our job is to learn why and dismantle it."

Watson was right, Caldwell had thought about the exact same possibility. No scenario seemed to prospect a happy ending, no matter how many times he played it in his head. It always ended up with him failing to protect Frankie, and delete the Android himself. "Commander King, what's his status, doctor?" Dr. Gillman divided the hologram into two screens. She showed the man's DNA, and although Frankie seemed right about the infectious disease, all Dr. Gillman had been able to do at this point was to slow the process down. "The degenerative condition has stopped. Between you and me, I could take him out of stasis right now, and have him work just like he did before he was infected." Caldwell smiled, but she added, "One sneeze, and everyone around him is infected. One cough, one cut, one tear, you get the picture." The room fell silent again. Caldwell, and King might not have been best friends, but he was the best security he had. "So, he's as good as dead, is that what you're saying, Dr. Gillman?" She shook her head, and added Frankie's DNA beside King's, and pointed out, "Somehow, twenty-first-century humans were immune to diseases, as such, because most humans in North America were vaccinated against Hepatitis. I know this sounds incredibly crazy, and it should, but the vaccines that Frankie got, plus her 'antique' immune system, seems stronger than King's. All I have to do is isolate what makes her resistant and replicate it. This is no Grey shit, it's a human gift."

"Dr. Gillman, you work on the DNA extraction immunity, whatever you said. Watson, I want you to see the Admiral, and try to force out whatever information you can get from her. We need everything, so we can know more about the Alliance's position in this mess."

"You, Sir, what will you do, Captain?"

"I'll hold the fort for as long as I can."

Walking toward the door, the Captain reminded them all to keep their mouth shut, and not to reveal a word to the rest of the crew. "Rats are always the first to leave a sinking ship. We need to see who will be ready to depart at the first sign of trouble." All agreed and left the war room.

Caldwell walked back to the bridge. "Sir, we received several codes from the Rake's ship. They are Alliance codes, provided by chips from Liberty. The other series of numbers are not from chips but are in line with Liberty." Caldwell ordered a clarification, "What does it mean, Cadet?" Zwally seemed perplexed, "Looking at the main screen, and back at my monitor I would say that Commander Stein is asking for us to use *Ra*'s Motion Decoder, and beam those people aboard *Ra*."

Caldwell looked around and noticed his bridge crew were paler than ghosts. He glanced at the screen, and heard Zwally ask for his orders,

## A.D WAYNE

"Permission granted. Turn the Motion on Cadet, and have them directed to the medical facility." His voice, ghostly, and monotone, the Captain couldn't believe what he witnessed before his eyes, staring at the main monitor screen.

"Aye, Sir." She murmured, "They materialized well."

In a moment of deathly silence, a robust rumbling sound was heard throughout the entire starship. "Report!" Quickly, his eyes lowered to Gillman, and Watson who turned around to stare back. "Sir...*Ra*'s being boarded."

# A COMMON GRAVE

## A Common Grave

Moments before *Ra* received the signal from Lt. Cmdr. Stein...

Crawling through the metallic vent, Frankie followed the feet of Leroy. Madsen followed on her back, her abs keeping her up enough to point her plasma gun at whoever would come their way presenting a threat. Frankie wished they would arrive faster in engineering. Suddenly, she heard cries, and loud, strident screams. Echoing throughout the intersecting ventilation corridors, everyone stopped, and listened to the agony of the cries from biological entities. Some had cracking voices, while others had high pitched screams, hurt by the torment the Rakes had brought them. "Where is it coming from, Leroy?" Frankie asked. "Left, two hundred meters down." She ordered them to go, and Madsen said with a hasty voice to Frankie, and Leroy, "Let's hurry."

They crawled down the venting corridor, following the Android. They were trusting that he would guide them toward the lamentations, which got louder, and louder as they approached. Madsen's species had a perfect empath sense. They shared a faint telepath link with others capable of the same. Frankie now had a faint telepathic ability that her Grey gene provided. *"I can sense Leroy. His emotions are true. I believe we can trust him."* Frankie agreed, and Madsen added *"His human reflexes are very on point. Right now, he's fighting high levels of anxiety."*

Aren't we all.

*"Frank, if Leroy falls into a PTSD episode, we'll be defenseless."*

Let's keep his mind busy, then.

With every knee, and elbow, the metallic cubic ventilation system echoed, the air as humid as ever. Frankie felt sweat pouring from her forehead. She was hoping it wouldn't fall into her eyes, blinding her with the saltiness of her skin. She heard Leroy say, "We've arrived." He unhooked the rectangular grid, and helped Frankie, and Madsen down. The moment Frankie touched the ground, she was hit by a wall of ammonia, mixed with a foul smell of yeast, and sweetness. As Frankie covered her nose with the inside of her elbow, she looked at the walls of the cell. They had been eaten up by years of negligence, leaving all metallic walls to rust. The humidity dripping down from the ceiling, she noticed some mold, explaining the musty smell she had caught upon when crawling to the cries from the vent.

The exposed pipes hanging from the ceiling dripped with condensation. Multiple gases were being released in the room. Madsen mentioned, "We can't stay here long, these will soon inflame our lungs." She pointed at the detained victims in the room, "Long exposure like theirs had them developed many respiratory problems. Oxygen is not getting through properly." It made Frankie wonder how long those seven people had remained imprisoned in the room surrounded by decayed bodies, most likely from former crewmates. She closed her eyes, afraid to open them, as she knew she now had to face those who were still alive.

Frankie took a deep breath and turned around to face the victims. She crawled over to them. "They won't be able to come with us, Commander. How are we supposed to save them?" Frankie heard Madsen, but as she looked around her Frankie saw bones, and flesh torn apart, like a dog who had enjoyed a T-bone steak all over the rusty hard floor. She lifted her eyes slowly and saw three women, wearing the Alliance uniform. Two were Cadets, while the other was a Lieutenant. Their costumes tattered, and covered in blood and soot. Frankie noticed two of them were missing their feet, while one had her arm chewed apart up to her shoulder. The only clean lines on the officers' bodies were the ones left by their tears of agony, and prayers to die.

Frankie knew how the Rakes enjoyed feeding on the living, excited by their cries, and screams. Each encounter *Ra* had with the Rakes, Frankie robbed them from their prize. She killed her own crewmates if there were no other way to save them. She would not leave them in the hands of the flesh-eating species. She looked up, and saw two men chained with their arms up. They had been regularly fed upon from toes to head. Madsen, credited with medical assistance, was able to keep her gastric liquid in her stomach, and helped Leroy unchain the two

Alliance officers. The other two men faced the back corners of the dungeon, and their heads leaned against the wall, missing fingers. Once the two men, missing parts of their legs sat down, they were unable to speak, Madsen ran to the corner, and said, "Their eyes were taken out, Sir."

Frankie felt a knot in her stomach, then a burning sensation, as bile began to come up her throat followed by gag reflex. *You're a commanding officer. You are in charge of this. You swallow your fears, and save those people, now, Frankie! Now!*

"Leroy, can you read their officer Alliance chips?" The Android nodded, "All right, configure it to match this frequency." Frankie showed him her monitor screen attached to her arm-bracer, and the Android responded, "Yes, Sir!" She ordered Leroy to move the officers, now declared deceased to the middle of the room. Once done, Frankie looked around for an electrical device, and saw an old crank that was used to turn lights on, and off. It almost reminded her of what made Frankenstein's monster's come to life. "Leroy, is it possible to use one of those conductors, reduce the voltage, and use it to mark the two left with a signature the Motion Decoder can read?" Leroy confirmed that using electricity to reanimate the near-corpses of the two left would be enough. "But it will work only on one of them, Sir. I can't 'electrocute' both at the same time. It would give two different signatures. The Motion Decoder will read them as one, and the end result would be horrific."

She had known what his answer would be, Frankie had half-way hoped he had a trick up his sleeve, but sadly there was no other way. She looked at the agonizing body, eaten alive by the Rakes. She now knew they were under the command of both the Dome, and Alliance. Frankie had no choice; heavy steps would soon be coming their way. She made up her mind. "Madsen, which one has a better chance at survival?" She pointed at the one in the left corner. Frankie unlocked the chamber and pulled the trigger: A series of bullets came out faster than the eye could blink, and ended the life of the right blind man facing the corner. He never felt his end coming, "For all I know, I did you a favor. May God have mercy on me, and to you, rest in peace."

Frankie turned on her monitor screen and accessed *Ra*'s central computer. In the tactical defense, she entered the frequency from which Cadet Zwally would be able to teleport the wounded to the medical facility. "You think they'll do it, Sir?" Frankie lowered her arm once the algorithms were sent. "We'll see in about two seconds." A cascade of light orbs appeared and swirled around the bodies. Each dematerialized before their eyes. Hopefully, back on-board *Ra,* where they could be treated by Dr. Gillman, and her medical officers.

"Now, let's move."

In the metallic conduit, all three started crawling away from the dungeon. The moment they heard the door open, Frankie held up her arm, and ordered a complete stop, and silence. Leroy, and Frankie on their bellies, Madsen on her back, looking to shoot at whoever would be coming for them. She felt a strange knotting sensation right where her stomach was going up to her throat. Burning, Frankie knew her stress level would soon consume her. It was too late to doubt herself now. She had to finish her mission at all costs despite her knowledge: *This is a trap, and I willingly guided three people right into it. Is Leroy even worth trusting?* Her eyes closed for a moment, and she saw Caldwell's frosty eyes staring into hers, when his body rested upon her own. A moment where the world disappeared, and all that mattered were the two of them. *Nothing else matters now, it's me that he wants, and he'll do it by taking him. I can't do anything without that converter. Shit!*

"Madsen, go find Leclerc, and Wolf, and leave the ship. Leroy, and I will overload the core from the bridge. I'm not leaving until this shit hole is in fucking pieces." Madsen refused. Frankie could feel why because she shared the same sisterhood Madsen did. Frankie knew her husband and her children. They always celebrated holidays together, had done so for over four years now, and there was no way one would die without the other. "A Captain goes down with the ship, a first in command goes down to save the crew. It's an order, my sister. Make sure you all get aboard *Ra* safely."

Frankie watched Madsen crawling away on all fours toward engineering, while Leroy guided Frankie toward the bridge. A little climbing through internal tubes, accessing a secondary passage to get to the main deck, and the smell of rotting flesh hit her nose, and burned her nostrils. She stopped a few times to drink water from her aluminum gourd and then kept going. She could now recognize the odor. The strongest whiff of rotten cabbage, and feces were always right next to the bridge, where entrails would be displayed, as a reminder to whoever dared cross their path. They would perish in agony to the hunger of the Rakes.

The ventilation modules were now right above where Frankie wanted to be. The air was unbreathable, and the weight of the heat wore her thin. Frankie was now ready to end the threat of this ship. She feared it was just a surveillance outpost, as she was sure someone had ratted on them. "Here we are, Sir." His voice, it shook, and felt unsure. His lips were trembling, and he kept wiping his face. She related to the feeling and thought to herself that whoever had put him together did an incredible job at imitating human behavior. "You know Captain Caldwell's crew are watching us."

"Cap...Captain Caldwell, Sir?"

"Yes. You seem surprised to hear his name. Earlier you mentioned he was saved."

Frankie made Leroy stop, and with her back against the side of the metallic vent wall, she had him face her. She desired nothing more than to know the truth of what was happening. Because the *Cerberus II* being a Trojan Horse, in Leroy's words, had her thinking about the situation they were facing, and what role Caldwell played in the scenario. This has been nothing more than a headache, chaotic adventures in deep space, in a fluctuating timeline. Frankie's thoughts were driving her to the edge of her sanity. Her stomach was roaring for food, and she could kill on sight for more water, her skin was sticking to the warm metal because of the sweat pouring from her pores. She took her Murphy in her hands, and pointed it at Leroy letting him know she knew exactly where to shoot to deactivate him. It was with a condescending, monotonic voice that she said,

"I'm gross, covered in blood and rotten flesh, ready to kill if it means I'll get a shower with my man, and I'm holding a gun.

Start talking."

The Android looked away, toward the grid that would allow them to land right in the middle of the bridge. Apparently, all the Rakes were somewhere else, and Frankie knew where, *Ra*.

"Captain Caldwell was saved by Colonel Locklear and Mrs. Borg, nonetheless, presumed dead according to Liberty's files. Therefore, he was filed as deceased by Alliance's documents. I thought Jason was dead, Sir." His voice was trembling.

"You, and I both know you can do better than that." Frankie's patience was growing thin.

"All right!" Leroy whispered his hands in the air while she pointed at the location of where a human pancreas would be, knowing her bullets would quickly get through and push the off button.

"Liberty is falsifying military files to hide the truth from the Alliance. The moment the news was confirmed that The Dome had allied themselves alongside the Rakes, the Alliance decided to retaliate, and change their tactics. Liberty's special unit military and the OWLS decided to come up with a plan to stop the Alliance. That's where Captain Caldwell came into place. He was the only one with the necessary knowledge to pull it off, because of his enhanced DNA."

"What's the Alliance's plan now, because we know they are working with The Dome."

"Isn't it obvious? They want you. They want me. They want Caldwell, and Alaska, and the entire crew of *Slicer*! We are the most dangerous threat the universe has ever known since the Greys. If we succeed, we can alienate the Rakes, The Dome, and the universe with our ship! Do you understand what I'm saying? The Alliance signed a treaty with The Dome to join forces to capture us! People are being pulled from their timelines, people that were once in contact with Greys, Tritonians, and Pleiadians, because they are feared to be part of Caldwell's crew!"

Frankie knew Liberty saved the Earth's rejected people once, and so they might be very capable of doing it again. Leroy confessing that his knowledge was given to him by THE man in charge, General Jones from Liberty before his last mission, had Frankie ask one more question that would clarify every single move she would make as of that moment.

"Why do I have this hunch that you despise Caldwell, and would stab me in the back?"

"Because I'm not the only one in your circle that despises him. Am I wrong?"

"Let's move."

The doors of the bridge opened below, and Frankie decided to move the grid, and let herself fall from the conduit network to the hard steel ground. Impaled heads, and human flesh hooked all around the full rectangular commanding bridge had Frankie almost throw up the bile burning her esophagus. She coughed and covered her nose with the inside of her elbow. Running to the security station, she wiped out some old moldy blood, and turned on the screen. "Leroy, I need you to initiate the autodestruct sequence. I take it you've spent enough time here to know the ship by heart by now. You fail this task, and I blow you up, understood?" Leroy nodded, "Aye, Sir." She focused on the tactical station, and read the orders given by Zachariah, as all ships kept logs from their crew, recording their every single word. "We have to go." She said with a ball of fire coming up her throat before shouting, "Leroy!"

She kept pressing the buttons to try to get the time everything happened. She received a message from Alaska. "IIBS-A1 II_3A_0200" Followed by a frequency, "284.2 MHz." Then, "Synchronization 5. 4. 3. —" Frankie shouted to Leroy to complete his task, or he wouldn't be decoded as she blocked his artificial DNA structure. She witnessed his hands moving faster than any human she had ever seen, and as Frankie looked over her shoulder orbs of lights already surrounded her body. Frankie shouted his name once more before she heard, "Done!" The ship had stood in perfect silence, but now, there was an echo of a rumble. Slowly, it filled with methane. The only sounds were those of the Rakes bodies falling, incapable of reaching the bridge to stop the auto-destruction of their outpost and Trojan Horse. Frankie closed her eyes but said, "AI Tactical Manoeuvre Beta 12."

"Aye, Sir."

# MAKE MY DAY

2400 Hours, 20th of October 2510
(Gregorian calendar,)
Milky Way Galaxy, Rake Space, Scorpio Debris
*Slicer* Decoy — *Ra*, Command Room.
Mission: Rescue Ship.
Ship status: Sustainable.
Crew: 251 — 2 in stasis, 82 dead, 171 alive.

The command room was locked down. Frankie materialized, along with Leroy, her team, and the converter was now in Alaska's hands. It was about half her size and empty. It had a glass dome and was shaped like a liquid gel medicine capsule. Holding it together was a black rubber-like material exoskeleton, making it transportable. It had a touchpad on the side with wires of different neon lights flickering. "We need Watson's venom."

"We need who, what now?" Frankie lifted her eyebrows, wondering what her best friend, Alaska meant by needing the psychiatrist of the ship. Leroy said with his silvery voice, "I said everyone on this mission had a part to play in the revival of this ship, and Dr. Watson is of an arachnid species, close to what you would consider a black widow. His venom is imperial to the functioning of the converter needed to adapt to the Grey's propeller system."

"You have gotta be shitting me!"

"No, it's chemistry."

Frankie's arachnophobia triggered, and quickly she felt an intense shiver crawling up her spine, grabbing the base of her skull. Her palms turned sweaty and couldn't control her trembling any longer. Frankie was done. She slipped her hand down to her pocket where she kept the anti-anxiety shots. Leroy looked at her injecting the liquid inside her body. Frankie stared at him, and saw his teeth biting down on his bottom lip. Leroy clearly knew what it was and seemed ready to obtain one for himself. She asked if he received any type of medical help while under Mrs. Borg's guidance, and the Android explained that medication was rationed. All he got was engineering repairs stating that organic people were their first, and foremost priority. Lies. Frankie could hear it in his voice, and noticed his character change by the way he followed her every move while holding the syringe. Any narcotics are addictive, and once enhanced to attack specific chemical releases in the brain, could be even more attractive to someone who knows the effect.

"You're a junkie, aren't you, Leroy?"

"An Android cannot be a junkie."

"Not a Type 4, which you aren't. You're a Type 3, armed with human flaws that were too realistic. Your programming allowed it to directly affect you able to camouflage your true artificial nature. That's why they replaced you with Type 4, Androids. Perfect in every way, but resistant to...Nakamo!"

Frankie's focus shifted to the Commander. She now knew how to take him out of his current status. She was about to run out to the door, when Madsen grabbed her arm, and so did Wolf. "Mind explaining your train of thought, Sir?" Wolf asked when Frankie stared in the eyes of Madsen and tried to contain the tears in her eyes. She had to say it aloud, and she feared they wouldn't follow her command anymore. "Leroy is the rat that's been following Caldwell since the very beginning of his arrival as a 'human.' While the torture he went under was true, we don't know how long he's been held or tortured. If we conclude that's how they got him to talk, they created an addiction to narcotics, not only to set the pain aside, but to get him as high as a fucking kite! He checks all the boxes of an addict. That's why you, Madsen, couldn't detect the deception. But now, the drug wore off and we see the real, Leroy."

"How long have you known this? Why didn't you share the information?"

"I couldn't be sure at first, and I needed him. Now he can fuck off for all I care, I know what he knows, and he won't get us anywhere. However, what I've known is that we were walking right into a trap by going to the Rakes' warship. We needed the converter, and I didn't want anyone to second guess themselves like I've been doing all along this mission. Outside this door—"

"Are Rakes, we know. We've been under your command, and have known you and Captain Caldwell long enough to expect the worse. We're prepared. What are your

orders, Sir?"

Alaska held the converter. The team needed Dr. Watson to make it work, and Rakes were crawling all over the ship, with General Zachariah at the head of the troop. Now that all was confirmed about the entire game going on, she looked at her team, and said, "This room won't be safe for us long. They know their ship blew to pieces. We need to stay unread by the ship, Alaska!" She nodded, and accessed the ship's command through the monitor screen. "Caldwell's been here with Watson, and Gillman. The heat signature reads it at about forty-five minutes ago. Right when we suspected the Rakes boarded." Madsen said looking at Frankie with a strained voice hearing the steps coming closer. "We need to have Dr. Watson, along with all of us, transported to the medical facility. Can we achieve it through this room?"

"Unlock the safety field under the holographic projector table, and everyone grab onto me, including Leroy." Alaska finished entering the code for them to become ghosts, and effective after their last transportation, "Once this is done, we won't be able to decode again, because the ship won't read us." They were holding on to Frankie, activating the PBU kept as a security protocol for people like Captain Caldwell.

"I promise. *Ra* won't be our grave but theirs."

They rematerialized near the middle of the medical facility, right beside the central computer of the room. Ready to point their weapons at Rakes, Frankie ordered, "Hold your fire!" Dr. Watson was present, holding himself in the right corner of the ceiling upside down. Frankie quickly looked away as her arachnophobia had her detect him almost instantly despite the night lights on in the room. "Have him come down and explain the situation to him. I have someone else to attend to right now."

All nurses gone, King was still held in stasis in the pod. Frankie ran to him, and with the touchscreen, entered codes to free him from the restraint of the chamber. Her focus on her friend, she gave him a shot of stimuli. The moment he opened his eyes she helped him regurgitate the amniotic fluid by doing the Heimlich maneuver. Frankie could hear his cough, and then all the liquid came out, and puddled onto the floor. Once Frankie guessed he was done, she grabbed onto his arm, and turned him around. She seized his face with her right hand by the jawline, and had him look straight into her eyes. "Tutankhaten" His pupils dilated, a blue light activated in the center of the pupils before disappearing, King shook his head, mumbled a few algorithms and frowned. Frankie caressed his face, "Nothing begins. Nothing ends." Commander King straightened, and his eyes flashed right before Frankie, who then quickly looked at Dr. Watson. He stated that her blood could save him, but that now they might all be infected. "We're not, Androids cannot spread viruses or any infectious diseases of any kind."

Frankie dropped her news on her team, standing straight, and tall. She couldn't compromise King's safety in the stasis, until she had proof of him being an Android Type 4. "His blood, his blood is infected! Dr. Gillman said that yours could save him because of your twenty-first-century immune system. He cannot be an Android!" With a smile in the corner of her mouth, Frankie said, "Androids have synthetic blood in case of an emergency not only to camouflage their existence, but also to save lives. The blood that is infected is entirely artificial, and unnecessary to his survival. To reverse the process, we only need to empty him of his synthetic blood. Madsen if you wouldn't mind." Her friend ran to King and began with the procedure to empty him of all residual liquids. "There should be about 5.5 liters of blood." She nodded, and plugged Commander King into an extractor, instead of using a slower medical procedure. "It will take about two minutes. Any other secrets you kept from us, Commander?" Frankie shook her head as she wiped her forehead, and looked around her. The room almost moved with her, and that's when she glanced at Dr. Watson, the arachnid. She hastily stopped, and involuntarily gasped in fear. "He was taken."

Frankie slid her hand over her mouth, the back on top of her lips. She closed her eyes, and felt the moisture building up. No. She desired nothing more than vengeance, and at that moment she decided it was time to plan their attack on the Rakes. She felt his touch on her shoulder. She looked over and crossed King's gaze. "I was in stasis, but my programming kept recording all that was happening around me. Caldwell was taken by the Rakes and brought to the storage unit you both visited. He is being held captive, and I believe we both know by whom, and why." Frankie nodded, "It's good to have you back, Commander King." She was about to tell him to take the cons, but he said, "Officially, I'm still in stasis, and a human. You're in command, Sir." Frankie smiled, and looked at her right hand, Madsen, and then to Alaska. Frankie asked if she retrieved what she needed. "Yes, I have the quantity I need to activate the converter and use it as a stimulus to finish the equation for *Ra* to be at full capacity." Dr. Watson rubbed his mandibles, and mentioned, "You know, you can use more, and create a weapon against the Rakes. One bite, and I can kill a Rake three times over. I only released about nine milliliters of venom per bite."

"Sold."

Frankie ordered Madsen to retrieve more venom, and prepare the shots. The rest would use the cloning device to reproduce more of Dr. Watson's venom, and dip all knives, and bullets in the poison. There would be no more waiting, Frankie was determined to take the ship back, and free the man...alien, she loved. That's all she could think about while preparing their weapons.

King mentioned that he still felt Captain Caldwell to be a threat. He kept murmuring how dangerous he could be when Frankie stopped him by saying, "Commander King, my personal life is none of your business, but mine. The security of this ship is at stake, and whether Captain Caldwell is a threat or not remains to be proven. At this very moment, he is an asset to *Ra* as well as our primary mission. I intend to keep him here as his knowledge is too broad to allow him to be taken alive. Am I making myself clear?" King seemed ready to continue the conversation where they had left it, but stopped, "Aye, Sir."

The moment had arrived. Wolf restrained Leroy to a medical bed, but Frankie said they might need his services, thinking of him as bait to attract the head of the boarding party. The Android Type 3 had kept his mouth shut since the moment Frankie had revealed his true nature. Finally, he said, "How do you know I won't turn on you, Sir?" She sneered, "Because I don't give a fuck. Either way, you're going out with a bang." She signaled Wolf to bring the Android along. She was fighting the urge to hug King, and say how sorry she was for what he had gone through. Feeling sorry for the time it took for her to realize he was an Android too. Frankie had to lead her team to achieve the impossible: retrieve Captain Caldwell. She also had to kill each Rake on the ship, leaving General Zachariah to herself.

"We cannot afford to become separated. We are going to the main bridge. This is where we'll make our stand. *Ra* is ours to defend now. If anyone is against my command, it'll be duly noted in the official log." Frankie looked around, but everyone had their venomous weapons ready, each wearing medical gloves to protect their skin. Dr. Watson's mandibles were already moving, but this time, Frankie overlooked her fear, ready to save her Captain, and her crew. As she approached the door, she murmured, "If we're going down, it's going to be swinging."

The door to the war room was situated on the same deck as the

# FRANKENSTEIN

bridge. The corridor seemed desolate, the grids of metal on the ground drenched in blood. Frankie regretted her decision of leading her team away from *Ra,* when she could have stayed behind to fight for the survival of the crew. Madsen reminded her, "If we wouldn't have gone, who's to say we'd be alive, and not being tortured at this very moment? Right now, I believe you saved us, so we could save *Ra*."

Frankie, like many others on *Ra*, had come to understand the existence of the multiverse. An infinite number of timelines that had her doubt herself despite the logic of thinking that nothing matters. After all, somewhere somehow, another her was making the exact same decision or the exact opposite. At that time, everything came to a slow-motion state like walking into an event horizon. She lifted her head up high. Instead of crawling the walls, she took both her Murphys in her hands. She kept her lips tight as she walked to the bridge. With her team behind her, Frankie felt strong, and nothing else mattered anymore.

Frankie was no physicist, but she wasn't unable to comprehend the theory of what *Ra* was capable of doing. Determined to save her crew and the ship along, with Captain Caldwell, she asked Alaska, to walk in the middle of the group to be protected by all of them. She held the converter, now armed with the desired juice, since the flickering neon wires were now steady. "You'll be able to hook it up from the bridge?" Alaska confirmed that she could. But, Madsen doubted what was

going on.

"No Rakes. The bridge isn't guarded?"

"I expect either Rakes to be on the bridge or united around Captain Caldwell."

"Either way, *Ra* took some damage."

"Not as much as their ship, and what I'm about to do to the entire fucking fleet."

The door to the bridge was open but there were no Rakes to be seen. The bridge looked like it had never been touched. Earlier, Alaska knew the place wasn't safe to materialize. Quickly, Madsen, and Frankie ran to their stations, and looked at what the Rakes did to the ship. Alaska was now on her back under the commanding station, and accessing the engineering through the main controls, and hooking up the converter. "Tell me when to turn on the switch, Frank!" Madsen confirmed the presence of the Rake alphabet, and orders, but quickly Frankie overwrote the entire commands, and entered the background system to hook the converter to *Ra*. "Now!"

The lighting of the ship switched from a dimmed cold white light to a bright warmer spectrum. A background sound was heard all around as though someone had turned on a computer. Then, a hollow sound detonated, and the main monitor screen appeared all in black. "I think it wants you to say something." Alaska mentioned to Frankie who then looked at the screen as she squinted her eyes, "Hello?" On the black screen, about fifty rows of ancient Egyptian hieroglyphs in gold colors passed at high speed, until landing on one. "*Ra?*" The computer answered with a grave male shifting voice from low to clear, "Canadian, English, twenty-first century. Configuring." It seemed as if *Ra* recognized Frankie's voice. "I am Ra. The conscience of the Pharaoh Battle Starship, *Ra*." Frankie was about to say her name, but the computer responded, "You are Noémie Laila Desmarais, also known as Frank N. Stein, ufologist, and last descendant of the Greys, sole heir to *Ra*." She closed her eyes. "Noémie died a long time ago, call me Frankenstein." The computer complied, and as she turned around, Madsen said, "You don't owe us an explanation, Sir. We are following you, and will fight with you, side by side, until the end, my sister."

Frankie knew the change in operating system might have attracted the attention of all the Rakes on board the ship. Frankie asked how many survivors were left, and for the damage report. "*Ra* is self-sufficient and constructed of regenerative materials. With twenty percent elixir in the converter, it is possible for me to reconstruct the infrastructure in less than twelve hours." Ten people dead. Frankie assumed Caldwell had everyone hide, "I count a hundred and fifty-six life signs hidden in the cortex on deck eight, and a total of thirty-eight life forms moving through the entire storage deck." Frankie calculated that those lives they saved might have died after all, while one life was missing in the hidden cortex, and she knew who it was. "I am not programmed to differentiate life forms." Frankie ordered Madsen to transfer all medical files to Ra. Alaska hooked the old programming system to link to the computer. Suddenly, a bright gold beam hit all of those on the bridge. All were confirmed throughout the ship, and focused on one chamber. "Jason N. Caldwell's life signs are in jeopardy."

"Ra, turn on the monitor in the cargo. Give me visual, and audio, please."

"Aye, Captain."

Ra complied while Frankie gasped. Before her she could see the storage room dark, and kept in low light. She saw Caldwell tied up to the same rack table. Needles were attached around his head through a strap tied around his forehead, and seemed ready to penetrate his skull. His denuded chest showed burns, and mutilation. Frankie held her anger and anxiety in check. As far as *Ra* was concerned, she was the Captain now.

"What do you think of my new ship, Frankie?" General Zachariah said with a sneer.

"*Ra* is my ship and responds to me only."

Frankie remembered Ra saying she was the sole heir to the ship, therefore, the only one in command. She knew the ship by heart, and said with a grave voice, "Ra."

"Yes, Captain."

"Kill all the Rakes."

"Yes, Captain."

As she turned her back, Frankie heard Captain Zachariah shout, "Do it, and you'll kill your sex toy too."

"Stop!" She shouted to Ra.

"Yes, Captain."

His voice, condescending, and reminiscent of a long-lost distant memory, reminded Frankie that he wouldn't leave her life so quickly, "You're letting your emotions take control. You're not thinking straight, baby."

"Bring Caldwell to the bridge, and surrender yourself at once. *Ra* is in my command!"

"Yet, you're under mine as long as I have Caldwell." Zachariah smirked.

Frankie walked to Wolf and pushed Leroy before the screen. She had him kneel after hitting the back of his knees, and held his head back. Her eyes fixed on Zachariah, her lips tight, as she grimaced with anger. Her muscles tensed, and unwilling to budge she shouted, "I found this piece of shit in your dungeon! Don't think for one second, I don't know how to bring you down. You, the Alliance, and The Dome." Zachariah's face darkened as his brows lowered, and so did his head. "Touch a nerve?" She asked as she saw him order his guards to untie Caldwell from the medieval rack. "You thought about delivering him to The Dome, and keeping me to yourself? If you fail, what will you lose?" They all vanished before her eyes. Frankie pushed Leroy to the ground, and looked around the bridge. "Everyone, weapons ready. They'll appear any second now."

The computer voice activated, "A Portable Beaming Unit frequency in 3, 2, 1."

Ra gave Frankie's team time to arm themselves, and they covered all corners of the main bridge. The Rakes materialized, and instantly two were killed by Dr. Watson's mandibles' bite. Alaska grabbed onto Admiral Heikki, ranged on the Rakes' side. General Zachariah held Caldwell by the throat with a photon gun to his head. About the same height, Caldwell's head leaned to the side, while Zachariah looked into Frankie's eyes. "Give me *Ra*, yourself to me, and I'll let him go."

"I've seen enough movies in my time to know that's the worse course of action anyone could take. I won't negotiate with you."

"Then so be it, Captain Stein. I might not deliver you, but believe me that Caldwell here is the most wanted 'man' all over space. You fucked the most dangerous Rake of all time. Congratulations."

Zachariah devoured Frankie with his eyes from head to toe, "I'll give you that baby, you know how to pick 'em." Her eyes were fixed on Caldwell, and she was about to shout when the ice of his blue eyes locked on her own. She felt a link forming, and a connection was made. All of his command codes, and his entire file transmitted to her as she murmured, "I..." She saw his lips move one last time, before the swirling light took him away. "You're mine."

# SO, SAYS THE PHARAOH

800 Hours, 2nd of December 2510
(Gregorian calendar,)
Milky Way Galaxy, Rake Space, Scorpio Debris
PLSS RA – 1332 A.
Mission: Temporal Battle Ship.
Ship status: Ready for Battle.
Crew: 159 — 3 in stasis, 92 dead, 156 alive.

It has been over a month now, since Captain Caldwell was taken alive by General Zachariah. Frankie felt guilty for losing the one male she loved with every strength found in her body. There was not one moment of peace in her mind, that his face didn't find a way to surface, and remind her of how she had failed to save him. Yet, Frankie had to think of her crew turning to her for comfort, and security. She had them work around the clock to help convert *Ra*, and learn its functions, and system. They had a place in the war to come, and she needed to brief them on the true history behind the Alliance, and The Dome.

It was now time for Frankie to face the music and awaken the one thing no one ever wanted to see, "a woman's wrath." Frankie put on her uniform. Made of nanofiber, the color of black, it had gold fine lines coming down each side of her body, legs, and arms. The one-piece suit had a collar, but she always left it open down to her breasts, wearing a black military tank top beneath, resembling a motocross suit. On her right arm was the gold hieroglyph of the Eye of Ra. One turquoise scarab pinned on her left above her breast represented she was Captain

Stein. Her black military boots laced up to her knees, and a holster hung off her hips, holding both modified Beretta 93Rs, the Murphys. On the other side, a Spider Gun, created after the success of her team, reclaiming the ship a month ago.

Frankie tied her hair up in a ponytail and looked at herself in the mirror before walking to the bed, where not so long-ago she and Caldwell filled the bedsheets with memories of affection, and loneliness. Gently, with a soft touch, she took his shirt, and brought it close to her nose to inhale his musky scent that she loved so much. Her eyes filled with tears, as she looked at empty space through the monitoring windows and reminded herself how much it hurt to love. She realized Caldwell owned her heart, and all of her. She would find him. She closed her fingers onto his shirt, and sealed her lips as tight as she could, and let go of his clothing before walking to the door. She was on her way to the bridge, and ordered Alaska, Dr. Watson, King, and Madsen to meet her on there at once. "It's time."

Once Cadet, now Lieutenant Zwally was at tactical, and Wolf was at his science station, they could begin. Frankie walked onto the bridge, everyone now wearing the original colors of the battleship, colors she saw from memories Ra had her seen: black and gold. Frankie said, "It is the Pharaoh Movement's Rebirth. Now, let's make history again." Her team on the bridge, Madsen stood tall behind her husband in the pilot seat, Frankie ordered Madsen, "Hail all the kingpins of the Alliance, and the Dome of the main sectors, and have them on visual, and audio. Zwally, prepare to bring Admiral Heikki to the bridge."

"Aye, Sir!"

"Let's make our entrance by rewriting history."

Brows low, her voice grave, and smoky, she looked up to the screen that quickly divided into six screens to show all the Generals of the main sectors from the Alliance, and two Governors of The Dome. Two of them were women while others were a mix of males, and females alien races. Frankie recognized many due to her share of information from Caldwell's ocular implant. They all seemed confused with their eyes squinting, and the sudden pirating of their secured frequencies. When King walked on screen, there were gasps and grabbing of clothes, while looking away from the screen that was locked, they were unable to shut off on their end. His appearance demonstrated that their plan had failed to have an Android Type 4 impaired. Frankie knew he might have represented a threat, and it was Zachariah's job to incapacitate him. He almost succeeded, and would have if it had not been for Frankie finding

Leroy imprisoned on his outpost ship. Deducting was Frankie's strongest suit.

"I am Captain Frank. N. Stein of the PLSS – *Ra 1332 A*. You, members of the Alliance, have attacked my ship, and compromised a mission of top priority, and secrecy. You, who swore to protect the innocents, and defend freedom at all costs, allied yourself with The Dome at the first sign of trouble. You were under the assumption that if you can't beat them, join them, and fuck those who would suffer the consequences. You are no better than those on Earth, my people and what they did a millennium ago."

Frankie carefully studied the body language of the Alliance's Generals, and saw discomfort below their coughs, and fleeing gazes. They questioned her authority as they asked who she thought she was to take over their secured channels, and lock their screens onto her. "I am Frankenstein, the only surviving Grey carrier. I am the twenty-first-century ufologist of Alpha Earth. I, along with my team, gave rebirth to *Ra*, and took down the Rakes' outpost in the Scorpius sector. I am your worst fucking nightmare. I am a human woman whose man you took. There will be hell to pay."

Her voice was graver than it had ever been, and her eyelids were so tense as she contracted her muscles. She turned her head over her left shoulder, and said, "Bring me their Admiral Heikki!" Meanwhile, she turned her attention back to the monitor. She saw the two members of The Dome sneering as she asked for the Admiral. Her voice lightened, "You think you're so much smarter than me, and yet, you're no better than The Alliance and as Heikki said you are desperate, and afraid." Their brows lowered, and Frankie got their attention. When they said they didn't know what she was talking about, she replied, "Of course you don't." She tilted her head, and with a grin in the corner of her mouth, she said, "You thought you had everything you needed from the night you planned on trying to abduct Colonel Dryden, but you didn't. That's when you realized you needed more Rakes. They were the only ones close enough to discover the equation, for what the Grey ship needed. You decided to ally yourself with the one race that is known to not be trusted." Her voice shifted to a low tone, "You failed." She looked at all of them, moving her eyes from left to right, top to bottom, "Don't think I don't know you are listening to me, General Zachariah. I know you are watching this. So, watch closely."

The door opened to the bridge, and Wolf brought the Admiral, captured after what the crew had named the Battle of Scorpio—The Nordic female had her pale white skin turning grey, and her hair was cut in a few places, shorter than other streaks. There was blood on her face, as her Alliance admiral suit was torn, and dirty from her days of torture in the brig of the ship. Fatigued, her lips chapped, and splitting, her eyes bigger than ordinary humans appeared gloomy. Frankie made sure all of them saw their Admiral before she used a swipe of her leg to hit her behind the knees. Admiral Heikki fell on her knees screaming, her arms splayed before her as she stopped her body from falling with her hands. Frankie looked up to those kingpins, their eyes wide opened as their brows arched. "You've seen nothing of what humans can do yet." Frankie growled.

She grabbed onto the Admiral's hair, and with a strong grip, pulled her head back. She signaled Wolf to give her one of her kukri knives, "The mistake you've made, Alliance, was to ally yourself with The Dome. Dome, the mistake you've made, was reaching out to the Rakes. You think that when you can't defeat something, you must join them. Well, I say, when you can't finish them, find someone mad enough who can." The knife was poisoned by the spider venom. With a confident and sturdy finesse, Frankie slowly pierced through the Admiral's stretched out neck skin. She kept pulling the head back. Frankie's mouth opened in delight, as she watched the muscles, and ligaments tearing apart along with the veins splashing blood around where she stood. The screams from the Admiral became choking sounds as Heikki drowned in her own blood, before the spinal cord tore free from her body. Frankie pushed her forward and spit on the lifeless form. High in the air, she held the Admiral's head in her right hand, her kukri in

the other.

Everyone on the bridge chanted, "Long live the Pharaohs!"

To be continued...
The End

## ABOUT THE AUTHOR

Born in Québec, Canada, Alexa Wayne grew up in the art field with thirteen years of acting and ballet school and multiple art classes. She pursued her dream in writing and graphic/web design until she enriched her education with Comics Experience.

She followed her dream of becoming an author by creating something unique: Gothic Bite Magazine. Alexa Wayne, proud French-Canadian, promised herself to never give up and bring in characters that share her path and roots. Her passion led her this far, and you can now follow her everywhere on social media.

CPSIA information can be obtained
at www.ICGtesting.com
Printed in the USA
BVHW030029040520
579057BV00002B/173